AS DEEP AS THE OCEAN

by

SERENITY WOODS

Copyright © 2017 Serenity Woods
All rights reserved.
ISBN: 1979744149
ISBN-13: 978-1979744140

DEDICATION

To Tony & Chris, my Kiwi boys.

CONTENTS

Chapter One 1
Chapter Two 6
Chapter Three 14
Chapter Four 20
Chapter Five 26
Chapter Six 33
Chapter Seven 39
Chapter Eight 45
Chapter Nine 51
Chapter Ten 58
Chapter Eleven 66
Chapter Twelve 72
Chapter Thirteen 78
Chapter Fourteen 86
Chapter Fifteen 95
Chapter Sixteen 101
Chapter Seventeen 108
Chapter Eighteen 115
Chapter Nineteen 122
Chapter Twenty 128
Chapter Twenty-One 135
Chapter Twenty-Two 143
Chapter Twenty-Three 151
Chapter Twenty-Four 157
Chapter Twenty-Five 163
Blue Penguin Bay 169
About The Author 176

SERENITY WOODS

Chapter One

They were late.

It didn't help Mac's mood. At two o'clock, he'd been prepared. He'd practiced his speech a hundred times, asked and answered dozens of questions in his head, and promised himself that if he was honest and open, everything would be okay.

By four o'clock, when the car finally appeared at the end of the long drive, his stomach was a bag of bees, and he'd convinced himself they were going to throw him out on his ear.

He stood by the fence surrounding the complex of buildings at the head of the vineyard, and jammed his hands into the pockets of his jeans as he waited for the car to arrive. His German Shepherd dog, Scully, sat beside him. She'd been subdued all day, presumably picking up on his mood.

He glanced to his right. The vineyard sloped down toward Blue Penguin Bay—a small crescent of golden sand inaccessible by land, and visited only by the occasional boat and the birds that gave the bay its name. The Pacific Ocean beyond sparkled in the afternoon sunshine. Boats headed out from the town of Russell farther up the coast, some ferrying foot passengers over to Paihia, others taking tourists to the Hole in the Rock or to watch the dolphins that would be playing in the deep water.

It was an idyllic scene, but it felt all wrong. There should have been a storm, with thunder rolling around the hills, and the sky gray with rain. Something should have been happening to mark the end of his world, but even though his emotions raged inside him, the sun continued to shine, warming the grapes in the vineyard and turning the terracotta roofs of the stone buildings behind him to a deep, earthy red.

The car—a taxi, he could see now—wound along the drive and pulled up in front of him. Scully stood, and he put a hand on her collar. Not everyone liked dogs, and some people found Scully's size intimidating. They didn't know that if you unzipped her fur coat, there was a teddy bear inside.

He saw movement in the car, watched the person sitting in the front passenger seat pay the driver, and then three doors of the taxi opened.

He'd been in contact via email with a guy called Fred, but three women got out of the car. Damn it, he'd assumed these were the Cartwrights, but presumably they were late visitors to the Cellar Door. He'd have to turn them away—he didn't want visitors here when the Cartwrights arrived.

To his surprise, though, two of the women began retrieving a set of cases from the car, while the third crossed the gravel toward him. Were they all sisters? Two of them bore the same color hair, blonde that shone with a reddish sheen like copper in the sunlight—strawberry blonde, wasn't it called?

The third woman stopped before him, and they appraised each other silently for a moment. She ran her gaze down him, as if sizing him up, so he took the opportunity to do the same. Above average height, five-nine, maybe, or even five-ten considering she wore Converses. Slim without being slender, curves in the right places, long legs. Her hair—darker than her sisters and a pretty chestnut color—was twisted up with a clip, untidily, with little care, lots of long strands blowing around her temples and neck. She wore dark-blue jeans and a stone-colored tee. No jewelry he could see, no earrings or necklace, no rings on her fingers. His gaze returned to her face, and he looked into a pair of shrewd hazel eyes. Fine lines touched the outside—no blushing eighteen-year-old here—he'd put her at late twenties, maybe a year or two younger than he was.

"Mac?" She raised her eyebrows.

He gave a short nod.

"Sorry to be so informal," she continued, "but you didn't put your full name on any of your emails." Her tone was vaguely accusatory. "I'm Winifred Cartwright." She held out a hand. She had an English accent, not quite Cockney, but definitely south-eastern.

Winifred. "Fred?" he queried.

"Yes."

He grasped her hand and shook it, his head spinning. The guy he'd been dealing with was a girl? He'd made all kinds of assumptions from those emails—had pictured Fred Cartwright as an acerbic

Englishman, a fast-talking accountant or lawyer who'd confuse him with jargon and smart words. He felt a brief flash of indignation that she'd been purposely obtuse, then remembered that she was right—he hadn't included his full name in their correspondence either. It hadn't occurred to him.

"I'm sorry about the informality," he said, "but we tend to be that way in New Zealand. I'm Eamon MacDonald."

"As in e-i-e-i-o?" She didn't smile.

"Er, yes. But everyone calls me Mac."

"Even your mother?"

"Yep." Her words were at odds with her tone, which was faintly hostile.

She held his gaze. Her eyes searched him like a flashlight, poking into all his dark corners, illuminating every single inch of his soul in a way he'd not felt for... years, maybe. Inside him, something stirred and stretched, like a hibernating bear sensing the arrival of spring.

The taxi pulled away, and the other two girls picked up the cases and came over.

"This is Ginger." Fred indicated the younger girl, whose hair hung in waves around her shoulders. Not ginger as such—maybe a touch more strawberry than the other two. A pretty girl, with finer features than Fred, although with the same bright hazel eyes.

"Fred and Ginger?" he observed.

"Our mother liked old musicals," Fred told him. She gestured at him and said to her sister, "This is Mac."

"Hi." Ginger gave him a flicker of a polite smile and shook his hand.

"And this is Sandi," Fred finished as the third girl approached.

He greeted her, thinking this was possibly the middle sister. She wore her hair loose, and she had a pleasant face and kind eyes.

Her smile was fleeting, though, and the bees returned to his stomach at their hostile resentment. He had a tough time ahead of him. Diplomacy wasn't his forte, and he spent his life out in the fields for a reason, alone except for the birds and the green vines and Scully at his heels. He didn't know how to put people at ease, how to smooth things over.

He lifted his chin. All he could do was be honest and forthright. That, at least, he could manage.

"This is Scully," he told them, gesturing at the dog at his side.

"An X-Files fan?" Fred held out a hand for her to sniff.

"Yeah." He was impressed she'd made the link. Scully, who was normally indifferent toward strangers, nuzzled Fred's hand and granted it with a lick, then snuffled at the others. That made him feel a bit better. Maybe things wouldn't be so bad. If Scully hadn't liked them, he'd have known he was in for trouble.

"Sorry we're late," Fred said. "The plane was delayed, and then, when we arrived at Paihia, we had to stop and take in the scenery."

"The photos don't do it justice," Ginger said. "Everyone says the Bay of Islands is one of the places to visit before you die, but I had no idea it would be like this."

They all looked across the fields toward the ocean. Mac could only imagine how it must look to someone who'd grown up near London. He'd been to the great city once, many years ago, when he'd done his big Kiwi overseas adventure. He'd hated it, as he'd hated all the cities he'd passed through, overwhelmed by the weight of its history, feeling hemmed in amongst all the high-rise buildings, the concrete, the filthy air. He'd felt like holding his breath until he set foot in New Zealand again.

"It is like paradise," he agreed, "and Blue Penguin Bay is the best part, although I guess I'm biased. I grew up around here."

"That's Russell, isn't it?" Sandi nodded at the town just north of the bay, a ferry-ride across from Paihia on the mainland.

"Yeah. It was the first capital of New Zealand back when the whalers and missionaries came in the early nineteenth century."

"The hell-hole of the Pacific," Ginger said. "We read about that."

Fred's steady gaze returned to him. "We were expecting less picturesque scenery and more prostitutes and bar fights."

His lips curved up. She still wasn't smiling, but he was beginning to think her sense of humor was Sahara-dry. "Only on the weekends," he said.

She treated him to a smile then, and, for a brief moment, everything went out of his mind except the two entrancing dimples that appeared in her cheeks and the light in her eyes that made his heart give an extra-hard thump.

Then she looked away, and his returning smile faded. She'd come to take the one place in the world he loved more than anything, the estate he'd thought was rightfully his until a few months ago. He'd expected to see out his days here, amongst the vines, watching the sun lift out of the ocean and fade into the hills until the day he died. But now he'd have to seek some other place to stand. It physically hurt to think of leaving. He couldn't imagine ever finding somewhere else that would make him feel the way this place did.

Well, you don't always get what you want, he scolded himself. No point in crying about it.

"Welcome to Blue Penguin Bay estate," he said to the girls, his voice gruff. "Why don't I take you to your rooms so you can drop off your luggage, and then I'll show you around."

Chapter Two

Fred picked up her case and exchanged a glance with her two sisters as Mac strode off toward the gate in the fence, Scully trotting beside him. Ginger raised her eyebrows, and Sandi pursed her lips. Presumably, they were thinking the same as she was. They'd known Mac was the son of the previous manager of the estate. His emails had been terse and to the point, as if he'd typed them with gritted teeth, fingers hitting each key with more force than was necessary. She'd pictured him in his late forties, gruff and grumpy, his face contorted with the bitterness and anger that the tone of his email implied.

And yet, when it came to it, he could have kept the news to himself and nobody would ever have known. But he hadn't. It must have cost him dearly to tell them what he'd discovered, but he had, and here he was, inviting them onto the land he must have been so certain was his, and not a lawyer in sight, nobody standing in his corner, fighting for him.

She hadn't expected him to be so young, early thirties at most. He was weather-beaten, in the way that men who spent their lives outdoors were, his face and arms a deep brown, the skin well-creased at the corners of his eyes. But oh, what eyes. They were the brightest blue she'd ever seen in a man, the color of the Pacific behind him, as if he was Neptune made real, or who was the Maori equivalent she'd read about? Tangaroa, the sea god, in person.

Just because he was good looking, it didn't mean she shouldn't keep up her guard, she reminded herself, extending the handle of her case and following him up the path. There were a hundred reasons he might have decided to tell the truth, and not all of them involved him having a heart of gold. Undoubtedly, something had forced his hand.

Mac led them through a gate in a tall fence, and she found herself in a large courtyard, flagstones forming a path through overgrown beds of plants, the palms and bushes in desperate need of some TLC. The buildings were beautiful, though, long, low, and whitewashed, with terracotta roofs, like those on the Greek islands, Ithaca or Skiathos.

She'd read online that the bay had a Mediterranean feel, and when they'd asked the taxi driver to take them first through Kerikeri before heading for Paihia on the coast, she'd understood what the articles had meant. There seemed to be more sky here, and although it must rain frequently—how else could it be so green?—there were apparently five hundred more sunshine hours a year here than in the south-east of England, where she came from. Cafés spilled tables and chairs onto the pavements, something she only associated with warmer climes, and palm trees lined the streets. Even though it was March and the start of autumn in the southern hemisphere—which was weird considering it was nearly Easter and daffodils were out in the U.K.—many people they'd passed in the towns had worn shorts, and hardly anyone wore jackets.

Mac headed toward a sign bearing the word *Reception*.

"I thought you might like to stay in the Bed & Breakfast for now," he said. "The rooms are all clean and have fresh linen. I'm still getting the main house up to scratch, but of course it's up to you."

"That's fine," Fred replied. He had a Kiwi accent, unsurprisingly. She vaguely remembered her father speaking the same way. The difference was mainly in some of the vowel sounds. His 'e's sounded more like 'i's. Earlier, he'd said 'yis' instead of 'yes', and 'fresh' became 'frish', while 'getting' became 'gitting'.

She wondered where he lived—was he residing at the house? She knew his father had lived there after her own dad had died.

Thinking of her father gave her a knot in her stomach. Harry Cartwright would have walked these flagstones, seen the very things her own eyes were seeing. It was the closest she'd been to him for over twenty years. She swallowed hard to contain her emotion. This wasn't the time or place for tears, not yet.

An arrow directed visitors to the right, where another large sign declared *Blue Penguin Bay Bed & Breakfast*, pointing to a long, low group of buildings. The whitewashed walls had been painted with attractive curling black and green fern shapes. The terracotta roofs made it look as if the buildings glowed in the afternoon sunshine.

"Oh," Sandi said quietly, and Fred exchanged a glance with Ginger, and smiled. When they'd first agreed to travel to New Zealand and see the estate, they'd decided each to focus on a different part. They would make their decisions individually, and, after a few days, they'd sit down and discuss whether to sell or to stay.

Sandi was to size up the B&B. With a degree in hospitality, and several years' experience working alongside the manager of a medium-sized hotel, she was ready to try something different and take up the challenge on her own. The Blue Penguin B&B had received unimpressive ratings over the past few years. Their lawyer back in England had told them that when James MacDonald had died and Mac had taken over, he'd closed the B&B until the girls decided what they were going to do with it. Sandi's task was to assess the facilities and see whether there was any hope of making it into a worthy business.

Ginger would be checking out the restaurant attached to the Cellar Door. This was doing slightly better than the B&B, and Mac had kept it open, but Fred had read the menus that he'd sent on her request, and she knew her sister's innovative flair would bring some life back to the uninspiring dishes currently offered.

It was Fred's job to investigate the vineyard itself. Six months ago, the only thing she'd known about wine was that she preferred red to white and two glasses were better than one. She'd done a lot of reading since then, though, and she was hoping that, with time, she'd be able to gauge whether it made sense to keep the vineyard or sell.

Mac unlocked the B&B with a key, and led them in past an empty reception and down a corridor. Fred could see four doors, two to the left, one to the right, and one at the end. Mac stopped by the first, pushed it open, and gestured for Ginger, who was in front, to precede him. She went in, followed by Scully, and Fred and Sandi peered around the door to look inside.

Fred saw a north-facing room filled with light, and a large bed with white covers. Apart from a few items of well-worn furniture, there was little else of interest in the room, no color, nothing pretty. She glanced at Sandi, seeing her sister's sharp eyes passing over the decor. No doubt Sandi was painting walls and hanging pictures in her head, giving the place some character.

"Amber aired the rooms and made up the beds with fresh linen," Mac said, moving on. "She's a local girl—the only one I kept on when I let the rest of the staff go. She's sweet—she'd be worth rehiring, although it's up to you, of course." He pushed open the door opposite and stood back to let Sandi in, then continued down to the next bedroom, opened the door, and gestured for Fred to enter.

He didn't move back, leaving little space between himself and the doorway. She had to brush against him as she squeezed by. He smelled of the open air, of freshly cut grass and sunshine, along with the faint smell of lemons—his aftershave, or real lemons? The taxi had passed them on its way into the vineyard so she knew they grew there, the first time she'd ever seen them on trees and not just in boxes in the supermarket.

She could feel his bright blue eyes on her as she passed him, and she didn't miss the answering tingle between her shoulder blades as her arm touched his chest. She ignored it, though, and instead threw her bag on the bed and walked over to the sliding glass doors looking out onto an overgrown garden. Paving slabs marked a path toward a swimming pool, which had been covered over, and was littered with dry leaves.

"The pool guy still comes up once a week to clean it," Mac said. He'd come into the room to stand next to her, also looking out at the view. "So you can have a swim later, if you'd like."

Fred's eyebrows rose. "Will it be warm enough?"

"Should be around twenty-five or so—the cover keeps the temperature up a few degrees."

They studied the view silently, and then Fred turned to face him. He continued to stare at the garden, so she had the opportunity to examine his profile. He was a good-looking guy, if somewhat worn, like a well-loved teddy bear that never looked new no matter how much you washed it and mended any tears. His hair curled around his temples and neck, needing a trim, and although his navy polo shirt was clean, it looked a tad crumpled—she knew he hadn't ironed it, had instead put it straight on a hanger when he'd washed it. His faded jeans had a small rip in the knee, and she was certain it wasn't a fashion statement but probably damage done by a stray nail poking out of a fence. He had no ring on his finger. That didn't mean anything, but something told her this man lived alone, or, if he was with someone, she wasn't the sort to fuss around him, tell him to get his hair cut, or mend his clothes.

His eyes were sad, and his shoulders sagged a little. He looked defeated. He was finding this hard. Fred felt a surprising twinge of sympathy.

"Thank you," she said.

He turned puzzled eyes on her. "What do you have to thank me for?"

"For telling us about the will. You didn't have to."

"Of course I did." His expression told her that he couldn't have kept the news to himself any more than fly. "I'm sorry." His jaw knotted. "I'm sorry for everything."

Fred opened her mouth to reply, but he'd already turned away.

"Take a few minutes to unpack," he called over his shoulder. "I'll be outside when you're ready, and I'll show you around."

He disappeared through the door, leaving Fred standing there, her stomach a jumble of emotions, churning like a washing machine full of colored clothes. She heard him call for Scully, and then his footsteps faded away.

Sandi's head appeared around the door. "What do you think?"

Fred turned to her bag, unzipped it, and began removing her clothes to hang in the built-in wardrobe. "Pleasant enough. Just bland, that's all."

"Yeah." Sandi leaned on the doorjamb, arms folded. "It's like whoever ran it before stripped all the color and character from the place. Totally unmemorable."

"You can change that, though, right?" Fred flashed her an amused look.

"Maybe." Sandi's grin belied her non-committal words. "Ginger said she's going to take five to freshen up. Okay with you?"

"Yeah. Mac says he'll be outside when we're ready."

Sandi rested her head on the doorpost. "What did you think of him?"

Fred unfolded a long dress and put it on a hanger. "Younger than I thought he'd be. And nicer, I suppose."

"Yeah. I expected some middle-aged grump. I thought he'd be really resentful, but he just seemed... sad." Sandi pushed herself off the post. "Oh well. See you in a bit." She walked back to her room.

Fred nudged the door closed and sat on the edge of the bed. Tucked in a pocket of her bag was a large envelope, and she retrieved it and pulled out the pieces of paper inside.

The top sheet was a printout of the first email she'd received from Mac, forwarded to them by their lawyer.

To the Cartwrights, (it read)

I write to you today to express my shame and sorrow at the behavior of my late father, James MacDonald. I know that your lawyer has explained the present circumstances, and all I can say at this point is that I wish things could have been different, and if there is anything I can do to remedy the situation, I will of course do what I can. I am willing to advise you as you go forward, whether you decide to take over the running of the vineyard, or to help you find a good buyer if you decide to sell, but of course the choice is yours. I will understand if you wish me to leave straight away. I look forward to hearing from you, Mac.

Fred folded the paper and placed it to one side. The tone of the letter had been regretful, but not overflowing with apologies. Mac had resented writing that letter with every bone in his body.

She understood why. Her lawyer had related to them what Mac had explained to him over the phone.

For some bizarre reason—maybe because he'd tried to put them out of his mind, maybe because he felt ashamed at having left them, they would never know—the only person that Harry Cartwright had ever told about his family in the U.K. was his estate manager and close friend, James MacDonald. When Harry had fallen ill from cancer five years ago, he'd dictated his will to James and asked him to lodge it with his solicitor.

Instead, James had drawn up a new will, forged Harry's signature, tricked another witness into signing it, and lodged that with the lawyer instead. The new will had stated that Blue Penguin Bay estate—including the vineyard, the B&B, and the restaurant—would pass on Harry's death to James. Mac might have been none the wiser if he hadn't discovered a letter from Harry to his children in a pile of old papers.

Fred extracted her copy of the letter, and placed it on her lap. She smoothed it out, calming herself before reading it, knowing it would stir up her emotions.

To Fred, Sandi, and Ginger, (it read),

It's been a long time, and I have no idea how this letter is going to be received. I can only presume that you all resent me deeply for leaving England, otherwise I'm sure at least one of you would have replied to my letters over the years. I regret not having been there to watch you grow up, but believe me, it was best for everyone that I left. I hope you are all strong, happy, and healthy. I, unfortunately, am not—I have lung cancer, and have only a few weeks left to live. You will discover that I have left the family estate to the three of you, as I never remarried here, and have had no further children. It is yours to do with as you will. I hope that at least one of you will come to New Zealand and discover the land of your ancestors, who have farmed this land since the first Henry Cartwright landed here back in 1820. It has been what Maori call my turangawaewae—my place to stand—and I hope it will be yours too. But if you decide to sell, so be it. I hope only that you lead long happy lives. Don't think too badly of me. I remain, and will always be, your father, Harry.

Fred folded up the letter and placed it back in the envelope with the other papers, biting her lip hard. He could never have known what a hurricane of emotions and events he was going to stir up when he wrote that. She could only imagine what had gone through Mac's mind when he'd read it. He must have been so tempted to screw it up and throw it on the nearest fire. Apparently, there was no sign of the original will. Nobody would ever have known what it said, and Blue Penguin Bay estate would have been his. But instead, he'd contacted them to tell them what had happened, and had told his lawyer that the fake will shouldn't stand, and that the estate was theirs.

Fred looked out across the garden and frowned. Just before they'd left, Mac had implied in an email that there were problems with the estate, but he'd prefer to talk to them face to face about it. There were so many layers to this story. It felt to Fred as if the estate itself was like a vine, its roots weaving back into the past, intertwining all their lives—James's and Mac's, hers and her sisters, Harry's and her mother's. So much lying and betrayal and pain. Would she ever be able to unravel the truth?

Well, there was no time like the present. Mac was waiting for them, and maybe he'd finally be able to give them some answers.

She went into the bathroom with her washbag, splashed some water on her face, then studied her reflection as she dried the drops with a towel. Unbidden, her mind wandered back to when Mac had stood next to her at the window, his fresh lemon scent stirring her senses. She couldn't think why—and she no longer trusted her instincts the way she once had—but she liked him. Oddly, he reminded her of her father. Maybe it was because they were both Kiwi men. She'd only been seven when her father had left England, so her memories of him had faded, like clothing left too long in the sun, but she remembered him as being down-to-earth, open, honest, and no-nonsense, and she suspected Mac had been plucked from the same vine.

And yet, obviously not all Kiwi men were like that. She thought of James MacDonald, and her lips pressed into a hard line.

For most of her life, she'd trusted her heart, but it was time to let her head make the decisions. Everything she'd believed had turned out to be a lie, and she'd be damned if she was going to let people play her like an old banjo for the rest of her life.

Feeling the need to freshen up, she kept on her jeans but changed out of her tee and into a white shirt. Then she released her hair from its clip. They'd had a few days in Sydney, so she'd gotten over most of her jet lag, and she'd been able to have a shower that morning, so the hair that tumbled to her hips was clean and held a slight wave from where she'd pinned it up. She added a slick of pink lip gloss to her lips to give her face some color.

Then she made her way out of the room and down to her sisters. The washing machine feeling had returned to her stomach, and she wasn't sure why. Mac had been pleasant and polite—it didn't seem as if this was going to degenerate into a shouting match, and she wasn't expecting him to be hostile. Still, there was lots to discuss, and she anticipated that he wasn't going to just roll over and give them everything—surely he would put up some resistance to them coming in and taking it over?

Whatever, there were three of them and only one of him. If anyone should be feeling nervous, it was Eamon MacDonald.

Chapter Three

Mac was leaning on the desk in reception when the girls came out. He noticed that Ginger and Sandi had changed into shorts and T-shirts, but Fred wore a crisp white shirt. The brisk look was toned down by her hair, which fell all the way to her hips in smooth brown waves. He'd never seen anyone with hair that long in real life. Somehow, he knew it would smell clean and feel soft. He could imagine the way it would fall around him like a cool curtain if she were lying on top of him, kissing him.

A light flush touched Fred's cheekbones, and he realized he was staring.

"Something wrong?" she said, her sharp tone belying her blush.

"No." He passed them and walked back down the corridor, Scully at his heels. "Let me show you around the rest of the B&B. This one's a family room." He opened the door at the end of the corridor, revealing a larger bedroom with two queen beds as well as a cot. Then he led them along to the communal room adjacent to the kitchen. "This is where they served breakfast, and where guests could help themselves to tea and coffee."

He stood back while the girls wandered around, brushing fingers across the dining table in the middle, the backs of the eight chairs, the cabinet against one wall on which bowls full of teabags, sachets of coffee and hot chocolate, and sugar sat next to a kettle.

"What's this wood?" Fred rested a hand on the cabinet.

"*Dacrydium cupressinum*. We call it rimu. It's an evergreen coniferous tree." Stop talking, he scolded himself as her lips curved up. She hadn't asked for a history of the species.

"It's nice," she said. "I like the color."

"Most stuff around here is rimu, or occasionally kauri."

"Kauri? Like Tane Mahuta?"

He raised his eyebrows, surprised she'd heard of the giant tree in the Waipoua Forest on the west coast, the largest known kauri still standing. "Yeah. You've done your homework."

She shrugged. "I did a little research."

Ginger snorted. "She read every single site that mentioned New Zealand on the internet."

Fred threw her a look. "I like to be prepared—what's wrong with that?"

"I'm not criticizing, I'm stating a fact."

Their tone held no animosity, and he got the feeling it was their standard way of communicating. As an only child, he found himself envying their casual bickering.

"There's a self-contained flat through there," he gestured, "for the owner of the B&B—you might like to check that out. And this leads through to the kitchen."

He led the way. To his relief, the stainless steel gleamed, and the clean counters shone in the afternoon sunshine. Phil, the current chef, could be a difficult character, but Mac had decided not to replace him because he knew the Cartwrights would probably have their own plans for the kitchen.

"Where is everyone?" Ginger asked, obviously surprised at the empty room.

"The staff has gone home for the day. Food is currently offered from twelve until three. I made the decision to close the restaurant temporarily in the evening when I decided to close the B&B." He turned away before they could query his actions. He had the facts and figures laid out on the table in the house. They'd get all the answers they wanted soon enough.

Ginger said nothing, but began to open oven doors and check out the equipment.

"She was head chef at a major London restaurant," Fred murmured to him. "So she knows her stuff."

"Was?" He'd thought the Cartwrights were only here temporarily until they decided whether they wanted to stay.

"She resigned a few months ago." Fred didn't explain why, so he couldn't tell whether Ginger had quit because of the news about her father, or for some other reason. "She's looking for a new challenge," Fred continued, watching her sisters stop to consult, their heads bent together as they gestured around the room, presumably discussing possible plans.

"I can't imagine this place would provide much of a challenge." He didn't stop the doubt creeping into his voice.

Fred turned and began walking toward the door to the courtyard. Mac reached it before her and opened it, and she shot him a glance before heading outside into the sunshine, lowering her sunglasses. He did the same, welcoming the feel of the warm sunshine on his limbs. Scully did a big stretch, then began to sniff around the flowers.

"For something to be a challenge, it doesn't necessarily have to be bigger and better." Fred walked slowly across the flagstones. "It just has to be different. She's had a difficult time—we all have—and we're all looking for a change."

He wondered what had happened to Fred, for her to say she'd had a difficult time. Broken relationship? He presumed none of the three girls were going steady if they were all talking about moving away. "I suppose emigrating to the other side of the world is a change." He nodded across to the view of the bay. "And I'm guessing this is a bit different from where you come from."

"Just a bit." She laughed, and her dimples reappeared. "We come from a tiny island called Sheppey in the Thames estuary, about fifty miles from London. The south-east is very built up and cramped. In its favor, it has a lot of history going right back to prehistoric times, and I think I'd miss that if I were to stay here."

"Our oldest stone building is the Stone Store in Kerikeri, built in the 1830s."

"My grandmother lived in a house older than that and it wasn't even a listed building." She rolled her eyes. "It's odd being in a country that's so new. There must be fields where nobody has ever set foot."

"We're all immigrants here, even Maori technically—they arrived in the thirteenth century."

"I've read that there's a pioneer feel to the place. Would you agree?"

"Yes, I guess that's true. We say we have a 'number eight baling wire' mentality. That was the wire used for sheep fencing, and early settlers supposedly used it for everything, because they couldn't just call England if they needed something. We're a resourceful people, used to coping on our own."

"I can see why." She bent to pull out a weed. It was the sort of thing you did in your own garden, not in someone else's. To Mac, it looked as though, in her mind, this was already her land, her estate. "It must have been odd in those early centuries, before the internet and mobile phones," she said. "Now, the world has shrunk, hasn't it? It only takes a day to get from one side of the Earth to the other. But it must have been strange when they landed in the bay, and knew that if they wanted to get home, it would take three months of uncomfortable sailing to get there."

"I suppose it made them get on with it. No point in complaining when there's no one to listen."

"I guess." She stopped by the door at the end of the path. "In here?"

He opened it for her. "After you."

"You don't have to open every door for me," she scolded.

"Why wouldn't I?" He frowned, puzzled. It was just good manners.

She said nothing, but her lips curved up again before she slipped by. Her hair brushed his bare arm as she passed, and again the hibernating bear inside him stirred.

Scully looked up at him, her head tilted, as if to say, *Really?*

"Shut up," he murmured to her, and shooed her in, letting the door swing shut behind him.

They entered the restaurant, and Fred stopped to look around. Mac tried to see it through her eyes—the cool, gray flagstones, the half a dozen rimu tables, the large windows overlooking the vineyard down to the sea, the roll-up plastic curtain that meant customers could sit outside, even in the rain. It was a simple set-up, and he could see now that it needed a fresh coat of paint, a touch of color, but he loved it, always had. He found himself holding his breath as he awaited her reaction.

"What are these?" She placed a hand on two large doors with hinges in the middle.

"They fold back to enlarge the restaurant if needed."

She continued moving around, running her fingers across the long kauri wood bar, looking up at the lighting, out at the view.

Did she think it looked tired and outdated? He felt a need to defend the place. "It's rustic," he admitted. "Not quite the top-class restaurant your sister is used to, I'm sure. It was never meant for three-course meals, more a place for visitors to have some snacks to soak up the wine."

"It's lovely," she said, surprising him. "The perfect location. I understand what you mean about the food being second to the wine, but it doesn't have to be that way. I don't think Ginger's planning haute cuisine, but she has some ideas for quality platters, sourcing fresh seafood, local fruit and veg, home-made breads, that sort of thing."

"Sounds great," he said, meaning it.

"I think you're right in keeping the focus on the wine, that has to be what the place is about, but there's no reason we can't offer some fabulous food alongside it."

"Absolutely." He liked that she agreed with him. He inhaled deeply, feeling the tension that had knotted up his stomach for months slowly beginning to dissolve. Even if she now told him she wanted him out, he'd know the place was in good hands. That mattered to him more than anything.

"This leads to the Cellar Door?" She indicated along the passageway.

"Yes. You want to wait for your sisters?"

"No, they'll be talking shop for a while. Besides, the vineyard would be my domain."

"Come on, then, I'll show you around."

They passed through where they held the wine-tasting classes, then he took her out to the main wine-producing facility, and showed her the presses, the temperature-controlled barrel hall with its stainless-steel vessels and oak barrels used for fermentation, and the filtration and bottling equipment, introducing her to the staff working there as they passed. Finally, he took her down to the vineyard itself, pausing at the edge of the rows so she could look across the fields.

"It's good terroir," he said, watching Scully bounding around on the grass, chasing rabbits.

"That's the natural factors, right?"

"Yes. Good soil, a decent slope, north-facing, great drainage, lots of sunshine. We have ten acres planted, and the estate owns another five that could be utilized."

"Why aren't they all being used now?"

"They were, but my father didn't pay enough attention to them, and we don't have the equipment or the manpower to maintain them." It was hard to admit, and he did so through gritted teeth. "I've concentrated our attention on the block that was growing well. We have six thousand vines and five types of grapes."

"I'm guessing Chardonnay, Merlot, Syrah, Sauvignon Blanc…"

"Yes, and Chambourcin, which grows well here."

"And the wine's good?"

"We've won awards, as I'm sure you know. A few years ago now." Before her father died. He saw her glance at him, and knew she'd guessed his thoughts.

"No reason it can't do so again," she said.

He made himself unclench the hands that had curled into fists. "That's true."

She studied his face for a moment, her eyes hidden once more behind her sunglasses. Then she looked away, back to the restaurant. "Shall we catch up with Ginger and Sandi?"

"Of course. I'll take you to the house, and if you're ready, we'll sit down and go through the books."

"Sure."

They walked back to the restaurant, where Ginger and Sandi were now wandering around, talking about possible plans for the place. Mac felt agitated, the knot returning to his stomach. The girls had been nice so far, but it was time to tell them everything, to reveal the truth about the estate and its condition. He'd hinted at most of it already, but he wasn't sure they understood. They walked behind him, their eyes bright, talking in low voices, their feelings evident in their tone and hand gestures. They were excited—they liked it here, and were looking forward to taking on the challenge.

He didn't mean to be patronizing, but he couldn't imagine these young women had any idea of the cost involved in maintaining an estate like this. A serious injection of cash was needed to get it back on its feet, and he doubted their bank accounts were overflowing. The last thing he wanted to see was them pile all their hopes and dreams on the place, only to have them dashed when they realized the little they could afford to do. He would have to be up front from the beginning, and make it clear exactly what a disaster his father had been.

He stiffened his spine and picked up his pace, crossing the courtyard to the house. Best get this done. He'd been dreading it for months, and it would be a relief to get it out of the way, even if it meant seeing the light fade in Fred's beautiful eyes.

Chapter Four

It was clear from the way Sandi and Ginger were talking that they were excited by the possibilities the estate offered. Fred smiled at them as they gave her a thumbs-up behind Mac's back, but she didn't say anything.

The place was stunning and full of potential, but there was a lot they had to get through before they made any decisions.

Mac led them out of the complex of buildings and through a gate marked *Private*. In front of them, the main house sat on a ridge of land, overlooking the fields of vines and with a splendid view of the Pacific Ocean. An orchard lay to the south, with lemon trees on one side and mandarins on the other. The air smelled fresh and sweet, and Fred couldn't stop her heart lifting.

Mac paused at the front door and turned to them. "I'm still in the process of cleaning up," he advised. "I was concentrating on the vineyard, so I'm afraid it still leaves a bit to be desired." Without saying anything more, he opened the door and led the way in.

Fred followed, curious as to what she was going to find. After his words, she half expected to find the place a bomb site, with walls tumbling down and holes in the roof. Structurally, though, there was nothing wrong with it. Like the other buildings, the whitewashed house was long and low, with a decent-sized living room and kitchen, and three bedrooms at one end. As Mac opened the doors to them, though, she finally saw what he meant. One of them was filled with rubbish. It looked as if someone had stood in the doorway and just thrown in everything they didn't want—papers, books, old furniture, frayed bits of carpet, pieces of kitchen tile, a clock with no hands, what looked like parts of a rusty bike, bricks, old bottles, cardboard boxes, a broken wash basin, even—to her disgust—stains showing there had been food rubbish tossed in there, although Mac had cleaned that up.

"I know," Mac said in a low voice, presumably seeing the look on her face. "I'm sorry."

"It looks like your room at home," Sandi said to Ginger, who stuck her tongue out.

Fred watched Mac's mouth twitch. He felt too bad to let himself smile. He hated this, she realized. He was mortified at the state his father had left the place in, and he was resenting having to show them with every bone in his body.

"This one's better." He opened the second door, and she saw that he was about halfway through cleaning it. Scully snuffled around, interested in something.

"Are there rats?" Ginger swallowed.

"There were. But I've had rat bait and traps down for weeks and I'm certain I've got rid of them all." He led them to the master bedroom and opened it. Fred walked in first and looked around. He'd completely cleaned this one, and it was a pleasant, light room, with a large queen bed and various pieces of wooden furniture, rimu again, by the looks of it.

It was tidy, but Fred noted the jacket hanging on the back of a chair, and the same lemon scent she'd smelled when Mac had walked past her. "You're staying here?"

He ran a hand through his hair. "I have been."

"I think the rooms will look lovely when they're sorted," Sandi said brightly.

Fred met her gaze and they exchanged a smile. Sandi obviously recognized what Mac was feeling too. They'd all been prepared to dislike him and his family, but now they were here, it was becoming obvious what a terrible situation he'd been put in.

"Come through to the kitchen," he said. "I'll make us a drink, and we can get started."

They took seats at the large, square dining table. Several manila folders rested on its surface, along with an A4 pad filled with slanted handwriting. While Mac filled the kettle and made coffee, Fred glanced at the notes. Most of them were columns of figures, but she saw at the bottom, underlined, the phrase, "Honesty is the first chapter in the book of wisdom. Thomas Jefferson."

She leaned back in her chair, watching him as he stirred the coffee pot, then filled four cups. There were no signs of a woman around. Why was that? He was a good-looking guy. Her gaze brushed down him. His shoulders were broad and well-muscled, the sleeves of his shirt tight across his biceps. That and the color of his skin told her he was outside a lot, in the vineyards, not afraid to get involved in the physical work. His past intrigued her. The fact that he'd reached out to them and admitted the truth touched her more now than it had in the U.K.

She still wasn't ready to forgive him, though. Not yet.

He brought the mugs across to the table, then to her surprise stood behind his chair. Scully lay down beside him. He picked up the sheet of notes and studied it, one hand jammed in the pocket of his jeans. His shoulders were hunched, his posture defensive. He was nervous. He thought they were going to give him a hard time.

Fred exchanged a glance with her sisters. Ginger raised her eyebrows. Sandi stuck out her bottom lip as if to say "*Awww!*"

He put the sheet down and shoved his other hand in his pocket. "I prepared a formal speech," he admitted, "but it seems stupid now you're here, so I'm just going to tell you what happened, and then you can ask me anything you like."

He glanced at the view outside, looking at the vineyard, where the ripe grapes glowed in the afternoon sun, then looked back at the table. "This land has belonged to the Cartwrights since the days of the early settlers, handed down from father to son over the last two hundred years. I grew up in Russell, but even as a kid, I loved it here and played amongst the vines, unbeknown to the estate managers." His lips twisted at the recollection of an early memory. Fred could see him as a youth, all elbows and knees and brown skin, creeping through the vines as he played hide and seek or some war game with his friends.

"As a teen, I spent my summers working here, and when my father took over as estate manager, I knew that I wanted to follow in his footsteps and be a viticulturist. I took a degree in chemical science and a masters in wine science, and spent several years travelling to gain a better understanding of the winemaking process."

He knew his stuff, then, Fred thought, impressed with his credentials.

"I came back from time to time and worked here," Mac continued. Then he hesitated, took a deep breath, and let it out slowly, keeping his gaze pinned on the table. "I hoped that one day I'd take over as estate manager after my father. I had no dreams of owning the land. And then your father fell ill."

His gaze rose to scan theirs. "You must understand, I had no idea that Harry had children. I don't know why he never told me about you—from his letter, I'm guessing it was because he was ashamed of leaving you behind. But as far as I knew, he had no family. He was diagnosed with cancer in December 2011, and he died in June 2012. It was very fast."

Fred clenched her teeth, refusing to let the emotion rising inside her show. Out of the corner of her eye, she saw Sandi rub her nose and Ginger look away, out of the window, but they kept their feelings to themselves, and she was proud of them for that.

"I was away when he died," Mac said. "In the South Island, on a viticulturist's course. I came back up when I heard, and asked my father what was going to happen to the estate. He then produced the will, in which Harry had bequeathed the estate to him."

His face was now like stone, frozen to cover his feelings. All four of them were very still, but Fred imagined that she could feel the emotion around them roiling and churning like the waves in the bay.

"I was over the moon," he said flatly. "Thrilled that Harry had passed the land on to my family. I knew that when my father eventually died, it would pass to me, and I couldn't have been happier."

At that moment, he turned and walked over to the window, where he stood, gazing out. "That should have been the moment that brought us together, but unfortunately my relationship with my father—which had never been great, although that's another story—took a turn for the worse. Now, I think the guilt had begun to tear him apart. He knew I would be furious and disgusted with him if I ever found out what he'd done. He couldn't tell me. And because of that, he turned his anger on me."

Fred hadn't expected him to say that, and she glanced at her sisters, who both also looked surprised and curious.

"My parents divorced when I was only two," he continued, still facing away. "I suppose I blamed him for the marriage failing, because he wasn't an easy person to live with. But he got much worse. Rude, aggressive, confrontational. He found fault with everything I did. When I tried to make suggestions for the estate, he took it as criticism, and just yelled at me. He told me he didn't want me running the place, not until it was my turn. He made my life a misery."

He turned back to them then and started pacing. "I'm not trying to make you feel sorry for me—I'm just trying to explain why I was unaware what he was doing. After a year, I decided I couldn't bear it any longer, and I got a job as an estate manager down in Blenheim. I worked there for three years. I visited Blue Penguin Bay from time to time, and I could see that it wasn't being used to its full potential, but I had no idea how far he'd fallen."

He stopped pacing. "I knew he drank a lot, but it turns out he'd become an alcoholic. He spent all the profits on drink, women, and expensive holidays abroad, while letting the estate fall to rack and ruin. I'm very sorry to tell you this, but for five years the restaurant and the B&B have made a loss, while the vineyard has only just made a profit. The equipment hasn't been replaced for years and is outdated and badly repaired. The place is in need of an overhaul, and it needs serious money spent on it."

Fred stared at him, and she could see her sisters doing the same. She'd known the place wasn't making a fortune, but she hadn't realized it was this bad.

"In the final year of his life," Mac continued, "he let the house fall apart too. I think he went a little bit mad. He used to let his dogs roam the place, as well as any other animals that cared to wander in the open doors. He never cleaned, and let food just drop to the floor." He stopped and swallowed. "I never knew how bad he'd gotten. I could kick myself now—I should have visited more, should have realized…"

"It's not your fault," Sandi said.

"Then who else do I blame?" he snapped. "I love this estate. I fully expected to inherit it, and I should have demanded to see the books, and to play a part in the running of it."

"It's easy to make decisions in hindsight," Ginger said. "I'm sure you did what you thought was best at the time."

His jaw knotted. He didn't want them to forgive him. "When he died," he said through gritted teeth, "I was relieved. Even happy. How terrible is that?"

Fred exchanged a glance with her sisters, then looked away. "We've all done things we're ashamed of," she murmured.

"I came to the bay with gladness in my heart," he said. "Walked through the vines feeling like a million dollars. The estate was mine! I couldn't believe it!" He laughed, but there was no humor in it. "And then I went into the house. I saw the state of it, and my heart began to race. I walked through the barrel hall, and spoke to the workers, who weren't shy in saying what they thought of the way my father had run the place. I looked at the books, and realized what had happened. I was horrified, and disgusted. But that's nothing compared to the way I felt when I started working through the rubbish in the house, and discovered Harry's letter to you."

He dipped his head, and for a moment Fred thought he was going to throw up. Suddenly, she could bear it no longer.

"Mac." She pushed herself to her feet and walked around the table to stand next to him. "There was absolutely nothing to stop you burning that letter and never telling a soul. But you didn't."

"That took some balls," Ginger agreed.

"I'd never have been able to live with myself if I hadn't." He frowned at Fred. "I don't understand why you're not all furious with me. I've hardly done you a favor. You came here thinking you'd inherited a dream, and instead you got this." He gestured angrily at the papers on the table.

"We knew there were problems," Sandi said. "You made that clear in your email. We're not completely shocked."

"We're a *bit* shocked, though," Ginger added.

Fred's lips twisted. She wasn't wrong.

Mac's eyes—as blue and deep as the ocean—were full of pain and anguish. "I'd do anything to change what's happened," he whispered, looking at Fred. "I want you to believe me."

She couldn't tear her eyes away. She felt as if she were swimming in his gaze. She'd known him all of an hour, and his father had completely screwed her and her sisters. She should be angry with Mac, because he was right—in an ideal world he would have demanded to be part of the running of the estate, and he would have noticed what was happening long before things got this bad. She was furious with James MacDonald. Not only had he taken the estate for himself, he'd practically ruined it.

But to her surprise, she couldn't bring herself to hate his son.

"I believe you," she whispered. And the answering relief in his eyes made her heart lift.

Chapter Five

Mac's breath left him in a rush at Fred's words. He had no idea why, but the fact that she believed him mattered more to him than anything else in his life. He hadn't cried for years, not even when his father had died, but now tears pricked his eyes, and his throat tightened.

"Come and sit down," Fred said gently, placing a hand on his arm. "We're going to talk about this, and see if we can find a way to solve the problem together."

"I'm going to have another coffee," Ginger said, getting up. "Anyone else want one?"

He nodded when she looked at him, and sat, watching Fred return to her seat. Sandi scribbled on a notepad, and Fred busied herself with pulling the manila folders to her and starting to look through them. They were letting him compose himself, obviously aware of his heightened emotion.

Scully rested her chin on his knee, and he stroked her ear. This was not how he had envisaged this afternoon going. He'd thought they would be yelling at him, prodding fingers at his paperwork, demanding to know why he'd made certain decisions, and refusing to give him the benefit of the doubt. That might still come, of course, but for now he was pleased and touched that they'd spotted his sincerity.

"What's the best way to approach this?" Fred asked when Ginger came back with the mugs of coffee. "Where should we start?"

Sandi put down her pen. "Well, obviously, I'm interested in the B&B and Ginger is going to want to talk about the restaurant. But we're both aware that if the vineyard isn't producing and making a profit, there's little point in having a restaurant or a B&B up here. So I think we should start there."

Mac nodded, glad they realized how it worked.

"So," Fred said, "can you run through the figures with us?"

He opened the first manila folder, and pushed the copies of the calculations he'd made toward them. "Okay," he said. "Let's start."

For the next fifteen minutes, he talked about the vineyard. He told them about its past, how big it had once been, and how he'd felt the need to consolidate when he realized the quality of the grapes was dropping because they were trying to do too much with equipment that was out-of-date and failing frequently. He showed them maps, explained about the various grapes, and discussed grafting of the vines and other technical information. To their credit, even though most of it was new to them, they took it all in, asking pertinent questions and discussing the answers among themselves.

"The thing is," he concluded, after much scribbling and frowning by the girls, "we're under-producing, and we're hugely out of date."

"If you had unlimited money and time," Fred asked, "what would you want to do with the place?"

He blew out a breath and sat back, letting his gaze drift to the window. "I'd buy a whole new set of machinery, and update everything that needed it in the barrel hall. I'd like to go fully organic, maybe try using sulphur as a preservative and clarify naturally, really haul ourselves into the twenty-first century. I'd double the Chambourcin plantings, because that grows really well here, and plant some Pinotage." He was speaking more quickly now, immersing himself in the fantasy. "I'd spend time opening up the canopy by removing more leaves to let the sun and breeze in, which would prevent mildew and help the grapes to ripen. I'd hire new staff, a full team, people who have studied and know their trade, and who would work with me to make this one of the top vineyards in the Northland."

He sat forward and returned his gaze to the girls. "I'd completely redecorate the B&B, make the rooms more self-contained with a mini kitchen and make sure they all have large en-suite bathrooms. Improve the dining room, maybe add on a lounge or a rumpus room with a ping-pong table and dartboard for kids. I'd get the pool repainted or even re-laid with a fiberglass lining, get a glass panel fence because the present one is ugly and restricts the view when you're in the pool. The kitchen's not in bad condition, but I'd probably extend it, make sure it had all the mod cons. I'd redecorate the restaurant—it's lovely, but it's tired, and needs a coat of paint and some new furniture. I'd extend the deck, and replace the awning.

There are so many things you could do, if you had the money." He gave them a hopeful look. "Do you have the money?"

Fred doodled on the notepad. "How much do you think we would need to do everything you've just mentioned?"

"Everything? I don't know. A few hundred thousand."

He could see by the way their eyes widened that they weren't expecting that.

"But you wouldn't have to do all that," he added hastily. "Not all at once."

"How much would we need to get started?" Sandi asked. "To get the vineyard making a decent profit? To get the place spruced up?"

"The equipment isn't cheap," he said cautiously.

"How much?" Fred prompted.

"It's difficult to say. Forty, fifty thousand? Anything less would be papering over the cracks."

The girls exchanged a glance. Ginger laughed. Fred sighed.

"I'm guessing you don't have that kind of money," Mac said.

"Harry left us five thousand dollars each," Fred said. "Plus another fifty thousand..."

Mac's eyebrows rose, his hopes rising. "Really?"

"That we can only access when we marry," Fred finished.

He stared at her. "Seriously?"

"Seriously."

"It appears our father had a sense of humor." Ginger's voice held more than a touch of irony. "He must have, because his own experience of marriage couldn't have driven him to do that."

"I don't know," Sandi said. "Maybe it was his experience that made him do it. Maybe he wanted to encourage his daughters to settle down and find the right guy."

"Whatever," Fred said briskly, "the fact is that none of us is even close to accessing it, so it might as well not exist."

"Fifteen thousand is better than nothing," Mac said.

"Maybe it would be if we still had it all," Ginger said. "But we spent part of it on the flights out here."

For a while, they didn't speak, caught up in their own thoughts. Mac's gaze passed from one girl to the other. He hated to see the disappointment on their faces. He stopped on Fred, studying the way her long hair fell like a waterfall down her body to pool on her thigh. She looked sad, and a tad angry as well. He hoped it wasn't at him.

"Could we mortgage it?" Ginger asked.

"No bank would lend us money until we were at least residents," Fred replied. "At the moment, we're just holidaymakers."

"What about you?" Ginger's gaze fell on Mac. "Could you get a mortgage?" Her gaze was challenging—of the three of them, he thought that she held him the most responsible.

"It's not my land," he said gently.

"Do you have any money?" she asked.

"Ginger!" Fred looked horrified.

Mac held up a hand. "I have some savings, but nowhere near what's needed."

"It doesn't matter," Fred said, glaring at her sister. "It's not Mac's responsibility. I wouldn't dream of taking his money."

He said nothing. He'd been prepared to spend every penny he owned on the place, but now it didn't belong to him.

"What do you advise us to do?" Fred's gaze was open.

He decided to opt for humor. "You mean apart from get hitched to the first Kiwi guy you see?" Their lips curved up, and he gave a short laugh. "I don't know," he said honestly. "I'm not a financial adviser. I suppose it depends how much you want the place. If I hadn't met you, I'd probably advise that you sell to someone who does have the funds to spend on the place."

"To you?" Ginger asked.

"To whomever you liked."

"But you would like to buy the place?"

He leaned back in his chair and played with his pen. "If you were to offer it to me, yes, I'd buy it. But in all honesty, that was never my dream. When Harry died and I thought he'd bequeathed it to my father, I did spend some time imagining what it would be like when I eventually inherited. But this land has always belonged to the Cartwrights. I'd like to work here, to be the estate manager, and to help get the place back on its feet. That's the extent of my fantasy."

Well, almost. His gaze lingered on Fred, on her womanly curves. He liked her gentle, elegant manner, her long hair, the way she lifted her chin when she obviously decided she was going to be brave about something. She was going to play a part in his dreams for a while.

"You said 'If I hadn't met you,'" Fred observed. "What did you mean by that?"

He shrugged. "I can see how much you want the place. It makes me sad to think there might not be Cartwrights on the land from now on. You look very much like Harry." He smiled.

Her eyebrows rose. "Do I?"

"You didn't know?"

Her gaze slid to her sisters, then returned to him. "We didn't have any photos of him in England. Mum got rid of them all." She studied her hands, her jaw set. There was obviously more to that story, but he sensed she was in no mood to share it—he would have to wait to hear her side of it later.

An idea came to him. "Wait here."

He rose and walked down to the spare bedroom he was halfway through sorting. On the left-hand side, he'd piled several boxes he'd already sorted through, one of which had contained the letter to Harry's daughters, along with some other of Harry's possessions. He doubted that his father had even realized they belonged to Harry—he'd just chucked them in here with the rest of his rubbish.

Mac ferreted around in them, and pulled out a small photo album, maybe twelve inches long and six inches across. He opened the album and flicked through the photos that had been slid into the plastic sheaths. He hadn't looked at these when he'd first found the album, too angry and upset at the situation to spend time musing over the past, but now he saw all kinds of pictures of Harry—from when he was a boy, to photos of him atop various mountains, because he'd been a mountain guide, to pictures of him at various ages with all sorts of people, whom Mac assumed were friends and colleagues.

But there were also some photos of him with a woman and three small girls, which must be his daughters. The girl with the long dark hair must be Fred, he thought, he recognized the way she was standing, with her chin lifted, staring at the camera as if to say *I'm not afraid of you!*

He looked at the woman, who must be their mother, and Harry's wife. She looked sullen—clearly, she wasn't enjoying the day out, wherever they were.

He pushed up and took the album back to the dining room. "Here," he said to the girls, and laid it on the table.

They opened it, and the look that appeared on their faces was a delight to behold. They all began talking at once, pointing at people they had obviously known back in England, laughing at the pictures of themselves. He left them to it, returning the mugs to the kitchen and washing them up, smiling at the squeals and laughs behind him. Gradually, though, he was aware of them falling silent, and glanced over his shoulder to see Sandi fighting tears, and Ginger hugging her. Fred's expression had turned stony, and when he glanced down he saw that she was studying the photo he'd seen of the girls with their mother and father.

He turned his gaze back to the mugs, and dried them with a tea towel.

"Thank you," Fred said when he eventually returned to the table. She closed the album. "May we keep this?"

"Jeez, of course, everything of Harry's belongs to you. I'll go through it all again over the next few days and get the other room sorted and cleaned. Then you can move in here if you want."

"What will you do?" Fred asked, lifting her gaze to his.

He shrugged. "I might stay with my mum in Russell for a few days until everything's sorted. Then I'll have to work out what I'm going to do with the rest of my life." He gave her a twisted smile. He wasn't trying to guilt her. He'd moved before and he could move again, get a job on another estate—God knew he had the experience and the qualifications. There were many vineyards that would kill to have him.

His gut tightened at the thought of leaving Blue Penguin Bay forever, but he pushed it away. He was here on borrowed time, and there was no point getting emotional about it.

"Okay." Fred put both her hands on the table and pushed up to her feet. "We need some time to think. How about we call a taxi and go for a look around Russell, grab some dinner, sleep on it, and then meet again tomorrow to start talking about options?"

She was speaking to her sisters, but Mac interjected. "My car's here. I can take you down to Russell and show you the best places to eat. If you want, of course. It's no problem at all if you'd prefer to go on your own."

He waited for them to reject him, to say that it was best they keep their distance, and that they wanted to take some time to discuss what he'd said, but to his surprise, Fred said, "That would be lovely, thank you," and Ginger and Sandi both nodded and rose to collect their things.

Acting as if he'd expected them to agree, he grabbed his jacket and wallet, then made sure Scully had food and water, and together they walked out of the house and across to his car.

Before she got in the front passenger seat, Fred paused and turned her gaze across the fields of grapes to the sea.

Mac watched her for a moment, observing how the light autumn breeze played with her hair. "Beautiful," he murmured, only realizing when she turned to look at him that he'd spoken aloud. He blinked, but she just nodded and glanced back at the view.

"It's incredibly beautiful," she said. "Much more than I was expecting."

He wasn't sure whether she'd assumed he was talking about the view, or whether she'd known he was talking about her and was just ignoring it. Either way, she smiled and got into the car, and Mac sighed, slid in beside her, and started the engine.

Chapter Six

Fred looked out of the window as Mac drove out of Blue Penguin Bay, along the winding road that led north through a thickly wooded hillside. Part of her wanted to study her surroundings, but most of her was conscious of the man beside her, of his murmured word, *beautiful*, that she was sure had been directed at her rather than the view.

He liked her. She could feel it. Could he also sense that she liked him? She'd only known him a few hours—there had hardly been time for any in-depth character study. But first impressions counted for a lot, and from what she'd seen of him so far, both in the way he looked and how he acted, she liked him.

It was a pointless attraction, though, and there were far more important things to sort out before she started thinking about her love life again. Besides which, her gut instinct had been wrong before, and she shouldn't trust Mac, not yet. He seemed genuine, but it was possible he'd vastly overestimated the amount they needed to spend on the estate to get it functioning properly, in order to discourage them from staying and encourage them to sell.

She risked a glance across, finding him lost in thought, an elbow on the window ledge, his fingers resting on his lips. Unless he was a very good actor, she doubted he could have faked the emotion he'd shown in the house. What his father had done had cut him up, and he was ashamed and guilty about how she and her sisters had been treated.

He glanced at her then, catching her watching him. She held his gaze for a moment, looking into those stunning blue eyes, and a shiver ran from the nape of her neck down between her shoulder blades. In the back, Ginger and Sandi were talking in low voices about money and the estate, but Mac's eyes made her feel as if there was no one else in the car, just the two of them, everything else fading away as heat seared through her.

Tearing her gaze away, she looked back out of the window. She mustn't encourage him. They were here to sort out the estate, nothing more, and it made no sense at all to get embroiled in something that would almost certainly end in heartache for both of them.

"So why's it called Blue Penguin Bay?" Ginger asked Mac. "Were there real penguins here?"

"Oh yes. Still are. Russell used to be called Kororareka, which means 'how sweet is the penguin'." Mac navigated the roads, heading toward the town center. "Legend is that a dying Maori chief said it when fed a broth made from penguin meat. They're still seen around the wharf, looking for mackerel."

"And dolphins and whales too?" Fred said.

"Yes. You can catch a dolphin watch boat—they go out to the famous Hole in the Rock, and they guarantee that you'll see dolphins or they'll give your money back."

"We'll have to do that," Sandi said.

"Mmm." Fred's gaze was captivated by the wooden houses, either white or painted in pastel colors, blues and greens and yellows. She'd read that it was unusual in New Zealand to see buildings on more than one or two levels, especially out of the major cities, which would account for why there seemed to be more sky visible. In England, bungalows were rare and usually more expensive than terraced houses, while their gardens often consisted of little more than a square patch of grass. From what she could see, here it seemed unusual for two houses to be adjoined, and they all had a decent-sized 'section' of land.

She'd known that her father was a New Zealander, and that he'd returned to his own country when he'd divorced her mother, but she hadn't known any more about the country than that. Her mother had painted Harry in such a way that the girls hadn't felt a need to find out more about him. It was only when they'd seen the letter that Fred had started to do some research. She'd discovered that New Zealand consisted of two large islands, that the capital was not the largest city—Auckland—but Wellington, and that the country was roughly the same size as the U.K., but instead of housing over sixty four million people, there were only just under five million.

She'd looked at lots of photos, and she'd watched *The Lord of the Rings* and had been stunned by the beauty of the mountain ranges and the breathtaking rivers. But, as Mac pulled into a line of parking spaces right before the beach and she got out, it was the first time that she'd felt any connection to the place.

She had vague memories of her father talking about the Bay of Islands. He'd always spoken about it with fondness, with a kind of awe and longing in his voice that she'd struggled to understand. But now she could comprehend why he'd missed it so much. She'd never been here, but it felt strangely familiar. Was it possible that love for a place could filter down in the blood? Reside in the DNA? If not, why did it feel as if she was coming home?

"Fred?"

She blinked. Mac stood by her side, hands in the pockets of his jeans. The sea breeze played with his hair, and he'd narrowed his eyes against the late afternoon sun.

"You okay?" he asked.

"Sure." She turned back to the others. Ginger and Sandi were also standing there silently, looking across the bay, and she knew they were feeling the same way.

She cleared her throat. "Okay. So where are good places to eat?"

Mac took them to a hotel on the waterfront with a large deck overlooking the ocean, and recommended the fish burger, which turned out to be less a burger and more a huge piece of hoki in batter with lettuce and tartare sauce in a bun, and a heap of thick-cut fries. While they ate, Mac told them about the history of the area, about the early settlers, the missionaries and the whalers, and about Waitangi, where the Treaty—the founding document of New Zealand—was signed in 1840.

"I read about some kind of issue with the Treaty," Fred said, polishing off the last of her burger before turning to her fries.

Mac took a swig of his beer. "Maori first came to New Zealand in the thirteenth century. That's the earliest archaeological evidence, anyway. And as I'm sure you know, Captain Cook landed here in 1769. Later there were sealing and whaling ships, and then missionaries came to try to convert Maori to Christianity. But you read about the area being called 'the hell-hole of the Pacific'—I think they were pretty shocked at what they found here."

"We think the original Henry Cartwright was a missionary," Sandi said.

"Probably, yeah. They bought lots of land in the Bay of Islands. Anyway, the English sold many muskets to Maori, and this led to tribal battles. In the 1830s, some *rangatira* or Maori chiefs wrote to King William IV in England asking for help to guard their lands. Eventually, a Royal Navy officer called Captain William Hobson drafted a treaty, and it was translated into Maori by one of the missionaries."

"So what's the problem?" Ginger asked.

"The argument is that the English and Maori versions aren't the same, and that, for example, to Maori, it wasn't clear what ceding sovereignty or governorship of their land meant—their attitudes toward ownership and use of land were different than the Europeans'. The meaning of some of the words is still being argued today."

"What do you think about it?" Fred asked.

Mac shrugged. "Some Maori chiefs were aware that they were never going to get rid of the Europeans once they'd started settling, and most of them appear to have thought the British were the best bet. I think the British meant well. Being a British citizen back then was an honor, and they would have seen it as a gift. Equally, I understand the Maori argument. It's not an easy issue to solve, and I don't know if it ever will be."

He looked rather surprised, Fred thought, as if he was unused to saying so much in one go.

"I can't believe we're really here," Sandi said softly.

Fred followed her gaze, looking at the waves lapping at the shore, at the holidaymakers walking along the pier, at the huge trees casting shade over the golden sand. "I know what you mean."

She brought her gaze back to find Mac watching her. He didn't say anything, but his eyes held gentleness and something else, an intensity, an admiration that brought heat to her face.

"Tell us more about the estate," she said to distract everyone from her burning cheeks.

Mac smiled, but did as she asked. He talked about the birds they'd be able to see in the garden—the tuis, the fantails, and the common myna birds. He explained that there were no foxes or badgers, and that the rabbits and hedgehogs they would see had all been introduced by the Europeans. He explained how there was nothing more beautiful than the sun rising over Blue Penguin Bay, casting its early morning light over the vines.

If he was trying to scare them away in the hope that they'd offer the estate to him, he was doing a very bad job. Fred could see how much he loved the place, but she also recalled his words, *this land has always belonged to the Cartwrights*. Even though for some time he must have felt exhilarated at the thought that he would eventually own the land, it didn't seem as if that was his goal. He loved working there, loved just being near the vineyard and doing his utmost to cultivate the best grapes to make the best wine. He was a viticulturist, and a Blue Penguin Bay boy, born and bred. Of *course* he was going to love the estate.

Knowing that he probably just wanted the best for the vineyard didn't help her out of her present predicament, though. While Ginger and Sandi talked to Mac about the B&B and the restaurant, Fred looked out to sea, wondering what on earth the three of them could do to keep the place up and running. She had just under three thousand pounds in the bank—not quite six thousand dollars—and she doubted that would buy even one piece of the machinery Mac had mentioned.

It seemed wrong to take over the place out of nostalgia when all they would end up doing was dragging it further down. She had no doubt that all three of them would work their socks off to try to make it work. And maybe that would be enough to keep the place ticking over. But the estate deserved more. Mac had said that the vineyard had the potential to be award-winning again. How she wished she could fulfil that prophecy. But hard work wasn't always enough to make dreams come true.

What was Harry Cartwright thinking now, wherever he was, looking down on them all? Presumably, he'd had no idea that James MacDonald was going to turn on him like that. Fury bubbled in her stomach at the thought of how the man her father had trusted, had thought his best friend, had turned on him, not only to take all the money, but then to run the estate into the ground. No wonder James's son felt such guilt and shame.

Her gaze fell on Mac again. His dark hair had reddish highlights in the evening sun. He was laughing at something Ginger had said, showing even white teeth, and laughter lines at the corner of his eyes. She had the feeling that in the past he'd laughed a lot, but not so much in the last few years. Why was he single? Had he loved and lost? Was that part of the reason why she felt such sadness radiating from him? Or was it all to do with his father?

Thinking of loving someone and losing them made her think of her mother, and her spirits sank even more. She'd promised herself that she wouldn't dwell on the past, but it was difficult not to. So much betrayal. So many lies. Why did life have to be so hard?

"You all right, Fred?" Sandi asked, resting a hand on her back.

"I'm tired," she confessed. "I don't think I'm quite over the jet lag."

"Let's get you all back to the B&B," Mac said, rising. He refused to let them offer any money toward the dinner, and went in and paid before escorting them back to his car.

They travelled back up the hill in silence. Fred was aware that her low spirits were probably affecting the others, but she was too tired to drag herself up by her bootstraps, which was what she normally did when she felt low. When they got back, she mumbled goodbye to Mac and promised him that tomorrow they'd talk more, then stumbled to her room. She just managed to clean her teeth before falling into bed.

"Fred?" Sandi came in, closely followed by Ginger, and they both perched on the edge of the bed. "Are you okay?"

"Just tired," she said.

Sandi brushed a hair away from her sister's forehead. "Don't worry. We'll sort something out. All is not lost."

"I don't know," Fred said, "I think it is. I can't think how we can make this work."

"We'll talk about it again in the morning," Sandi said.

"Mac likes you," Ginger announced, her lips curving up.

Fred rolled away from them and buried her face in the pillow. "Goodnight."

Ginger sighed, and the two of them rose. "Sleep tight," Ginger whispered, and they went out.

Fred was asleep within minutes of them closing the door.

Chapter Seven

Mac was cooking breakfast in the B&B's kitchen when Fred came out the next morning.

He stopped in the act of scrambling the eggs and stared at her. She'd braided her gorgeous chestnut hair into a long plait that fell over her shoulder and down to her waist, while several long strands curled around her face. Her cheek bore the imprint of a crease from her pillow case, and her eyes had dark shadows underneath. She wore a black T-shirt and denim shorts, exposing a pair of shapely legs. All she needed was to be wearing his shirt and the look would have been complete.

She bent and scratched Scully's ear. The dog licked her hand. "Morning," she said.

"Morning." He returned to scrambling the eggs, trying to ignore the sexual interest that rippled through him. "How did you sleep?"

She shrugged and came to stand next to him, her arm brushing his as she looked into the saucepan. "Are you cooking us breakfast?"

"It seemed like the polite thing to do. The kitchen crew doesn't get here until eleven."

"Aw. That's sweet." She smiled up at him.

"It's the least I can do." He made the mistake of glancing at her, and was instantly snared by her gaze. He looked into her hazel eyes, noting how they were mainly green, but had an amber ring around the iris. Her mouth was free of gloss, her bare lips soft and kissable, and he had to fight not to bend his head and touch his lips to hers.

He turned to the other pan, where rashers of bacon sizzled merrily, and poked it with the spoon.

Fred cleared her throat. "I want to tell you that I'd like you to play a part in wherever we go from here. I'm not sure what we're going to do yet, but whether we go or whether we stay, I hope you'll stick around to help us out."

He poked the bacon again, then glanced at her. "It's more than I'd hoped for, and I'm not sure I deserve it."

"Maybe if I get to know you better I'll agree with that, but for now I think you're being a bit harsh on yourself."

She was teasing him again. It must be his imagination, but it felt as if the sun shone brighter whenever she smiled.

"Are you feeling better this morning?" he asked, conscious that the worried crease between her eyebrows had vanished.

She walked to the large fridge, opened it, and studied the contents. "I was very tired last night, and a bit down. I had a few bad dreams. The news about the estate needing such an injection of money was a shock, and I still don't know what we're going to do, but I feel more positive this morning anyway." She extracted a carton of orange juice and started pouring some into a glass. "Did you have any bright ideas in the night?"

As it happened, he *had* come up with an idea, but he'd discarded it as ridiculous, and there was no way he'd give voice to the notion. "Unfortunately not."

She sighed and placed the carton back in the fridge. "Me neither."

"So what's your plan of action?"

"I think it would be silly to make a decision immediately, and maybe we should take a couple of days to let it all sink in and think about it. This morning the three of us should spend a bit more time on the areas we're interested in, so maybe Ginger could talk with the kitchen crew and find out more about the running of the place, and Sandi could draw up some plans for the B&B and come up with a better idea of what we would need to spend there to make it profitable. I know that the vineyard is technically more important than either of these, but if we were to find a way to fight for it, they would have to feel their part is worth it."

"Yeah." He took the toast out of the toaster and distributed it onto three plates, then began buttering them.

"This morning you and I could take a walk around the vineyard." She sipped her orange juice. "I've been doing a lot of reading about winemaking, but it would be good to hear more about it from a professional."

He liked the way she called him that. "Sure."

"I understood what you were saying about wanting an overhaul and replacing everything, but that's obviously not going to be practical, so it would be good to look at what has to be replaced, versus what you'd like to be replaced, and see what the cost of that is."

He started to dish up the eggs. The idea of just patching up the place made his heart sink, but she was right—in the absence of any serious investment, they would have to do the best they could.

"You're not joining us?" She gestured at the three plates.

"I've already eaten. I'm going to do a walk around, and then I'll come back for you when you're done."

"All right," she said softly. "Thank you."

"No worries." He picked up two of the plates and she took the third, and they carried them through to the dining room, Scully at their heels.

Ginger came in at that moment, yawning, her strawberry-blonde hair ruffled, her eyes sleepy. She perked up at the sight of the bacon and eggs. "Oh! Breakfast. Thank you." She smiled at him. Maybe she'd softened toward him, too.

"Where's Sandi?" Fred placed her plate on the table and Mac did the same. He went back into the kitchen to fetch the coffee pot and the orange juice, hearing Ginger say, "She's just coming," before bringing the drinks back into the dining room.

"Cups and glasses there," he gestured at the rack on the cabinet, "sugar there, help yourself to anything else you want from the kitchen. I'll be in the barrel hall when you're ready, Fred."

"Okay." She flashed him a smile and sat, and he left her tucking into her eggs.

Knowing Scully was hoping for a dropped bit of bacon, he took the dog with him and walked around the edge of the vineyard, enjoying the peace in the early morning sun. Occasionally, he stopped to check the vines, taking out some of the top leaves to let the sun's rays penetrate to the lower branches, but his mind was only half on the job. The rest of it thought about the Cartwright girls, and specifically, about Fred.

What was going to happen to the estate? Were they likely to stick around? He chewed his lip as he reached the edge of the vineyard, and turned to look across the bay. He liked the girls, and wanted them to stay, but equally if they had no money he couldn't see the vineyard's situation improving. They'd begin with enthusiasm, thinking they could do wonders with the small amount of cash they had, providing they backed it up with hard work. Then, as the months and years passed, they'd grow frustrated as sales declined, as the vineyard failed to win awards, as visitors stopped coming, and those who did left reviews on the tourist sites commenting on the mediocre wine and the dated B&B.

Perhaps it was an overly gloomy outlook, but he'd seen it happen before. And the girls weren't from here. When the first glow of emigrating wore off, they'd start to miss their home, and they'd blame their misfortune on the country. One by one they'd drift back, leaving the estate in a worse condition than they found it, possibly even irretrievable.

He should have begun with an offer, told them he'd happily take it off their hands, give them the cash, and send them on their merry way several hundred thousand dollars richer. He wouldn't have had a problem getting a loan from the bank, and then Blue Penguin Bay vineyard would have been his to do with as he wanted.

But he just couldn't do it. His father had ruined the place, and it felt like the ultimate insult for him to use the decayed nature of the estate as leverage to make them sell. They deserved more, and if they wanted to make a go of it, and they wanted him to stay, he'd do so, if only to make himself feel better.

But it wasn't just that, of course. He watched the boats heading out toward the horizon, and felt a warmth spread through him that had nothing to do with the sun coating him in gold. He loved it here, and he'd do anything to stay and help the girls make the place successful again.

He checked his watch—it was nearly nine, and he'd told Fred he'd be in the barrel hall when she'd finished her breakfast. So he walked back through the vineyard and into the hall, and spent ten minutes checking out the equipment before Fred appeared.

She'd changed into a pair of dark brown casual trousers and a cream blouse, and wore a straw hat as protection against the strong New Zealand sun, the long braid falling down her back like Rapunzel's.

"Ready?" he asked.

She nodded. "Ginger and Sandi are going to spend some time in the B&B and restaurant, so it's just us."

He wasn't disappointed with that. "Come on, then."

This time, he took much longer to show her around. He went into more detail about the different grapes, explaining what grew well and what didn't, and showed her some of the machinery that they used—the outdated sprayers, the too-small trimmer and defoliator, the pruner, all of which had been damaged and repaired numerous times.

He told her more about the terroir, and encouraged her to get into the rows of vines so she could see and feel the leaves and the grapes, which was as important to him as understanding the science behind why the vines grew. He watched her pop the dark-blue Merlot grapes in her mouth, loving the way her face lit up with a smile when he told her the word Merlot meant 'the little blackbird' in French.

In the barrel hall, he let her talk to the staff, who were honest about the quality of the crushers and the quantity of the oak barrels. The filtration equipment was okay, but he showed her how the bottling process could be improved.

Fred asked lots of questions and made heaps of notes on her iPad. She'd obviously done her research, and he was impressed at her knowledge considering she didn't have a background in winemaking.

It was with some surprise that he saw it was nearly midday by the time they'd finished.

"So we basically need more of everything?" she said when he eventually led her back out into the sunlight. "More machines, more staff?"

"It's not just quantity. It's quality too. Dad employed lots of people from the town, and that's okay—it's good to be a source of local employment. But most of them don't have any experience. We need to spend time and money on getting them trained, so they understand more about the winemaking process. And we pay shit, too. You pay peanuts…"

"… you get monkeys," Fred finished. "Yeah, I get it." Her voice was flat.

He ran a hand through his hair. "Look, I didn't mean to bring you down, but I wouldn't feel as if I was being honest if I didn't tell it like it is."

"No, you're perfectly right." She led the way over to a bench in the garden and sat, and he took a seat beside her. Scully sat on her foot, and she laughed and stroked the dog's head. "The thing is, for Ginger, Sandi, and me, coming here is like a new beginning. All three of us have had a tough time over the last few years."

"Because of your father?" he asked. He didn't want to force her to talk, but he was curious about the Cartwright girls, and why all of them felt the need to escape.

Fred leaned back, her hands folded in her lap. "Sandi's partner died a year ago in a car crash."

"Shit," he said. She was only in her late twenties.

"Yeah," Fred said. "She's still not over it. It was horrible, and not just because he died. At the funeral, another woman turned up with a two-year-old kid. Turns out she was married to him."

Mac's eyes widened. "What?"

"He was a sales rep, and he told both of them he was away a lot on business. When he wasn't with one, he was with the other, and neither of them knew. But of course, the worst thing was that the other woman was his wife. Sandi's house was in Brodie's name, so she didn't have a leg to stand on. The wife threw her out, and Sandi lost everything."

"Jesus."

"Yeah. It was a terrible time, and she's still reeling."

"What about Ginger?" he said, almost not wanting to ask.

"She had an affair with the son of the woman who owned the restaurant she was working at. He turned out to be a pig, and when she dumped him, he told his mother that Ginger was creaming money off the profits, and she was sacked."

"Ah, jeez."

"Ginger took her to court and won, but it was horrible for her."

The thought of people hurting these young, beautiful women gave him a pain in his chest. "And you?" he asked softly. Perhaps she'd only wanted to get away to help her sisters. He was conscious though that she hadn't mentioned her mother yet. Was she still alive? What had happened there?

Chapter Eight

Fred concentrated on stroking Scully's ears so she didn't have to look at him.

She hadn't planned to offload like this. She didn't particularly want to admit her failings, or those of her sisters, but there was something about Mac that made her want to confess. It could have been those eyes—they seemed to see right inside her, as if she were a museum piece behind glass, and he was just standing there, studying it.

She didn't want to confess everything, though, because she liked the way he looked at her, and she didn't want it to change. Still, he'd opened up to her. It would be rude to say nothing. She didn't have to tell him everything.

"There was no catastrophe for me in that way," she said. "It was a downward spiral of events that led to me being desperate to get away. My mother was bipolar. Badly so. She had severe bipolar I disorder. Do you know much about it?"

"Not much," he said.

"When we were young, I thought she was just energetic and exciting. She'd decide on a whim to take us all to London to visit Madame Tussauds, or down to the West Country for a sudden holiday. At the time, I didn't connect those manic episodes with the periods of depression that followed. As I grew older though, I began to see a pattern, and she grew worse. She'd drag us out for the day, then halfway through she'd withdraw into herself, shaking and uncommunicative, and I'd have to find a way to get us home. She swung more quickly from one state to another. She'd go on shopping sprees and she ran up huge credit bills. She slept around, even when my father was still home. She was hospitalized several times. She even began to have psychotic episodes—delusions and hallucinations. It wasn't her fault. But it was very hard."

"When did your father leave?" Mac asked. He was sitting very close to her, his arm brushing hers. Fred liked the contact. It had been a while since she'd been close to a man, and his presence comforted her, warmed her through.

"When I was seven. I can remember bits and pieces about him, but Sandi was only five, and Ginger only three, so they can't remember him much. I can recall lots of arguments, shouting, tears. My Dad pleading, begging her to get help, her refusing, saying she didn't need it. And I remember that she forgot to pick Sandi and me up from school one day, so Dad came to get us, and when he got home she was in bed with another man, with Ginger asleep in the corner. That was it for him, I think. He left soon after."

"He just walked out? I'm surprised he didn't try to get custody of you." Mac was frowning—he disapproved. She liked that.

"Well, you know he was a mountain guide, right? His job took him all over the world. He went off and came back several times, but Mum refused to let him see us. And then of course he had his big accident and hurt his leg, and he obviously decided he needed to settle down, and he moved back here."

"Did he contact you at all?"

Fred blew out another breath. "Well, that's the crux of the matter. We didn't get a single letter from him. We were used to him being away, but as the years went by and we heard nothing, we all got upset and resentful. Mum told us that he couldn't care for us very much if he couldn't even bother to write a letter. I wanted to ring, but she said she didn't have his phone number. In the end, I wrote to him several times, but never heard back, so I assumed he'd abandoned us and didn't want to know. I thought he'd probably remarried and had a new family. I hated him for that. I blamed him for everything. It was only when he died and you sent that letter that I found out Mum had destroyed all his letters, and all my letters to him."

"Jesus." Mac leaned forward, his elbows on his knees. "And all that time Harry thought you didn't want anything to do with him."

"Yes." Emotion was starting to stir inside her. She didn't want to say any more. She wasn't ready. She didn't know him well enough, and it wasn't the kind of thing you admitted to a stranger.

They sat in silence for a while, Fred with her hands clenched, her knuckles white, as she waited for him to ask. *You spoke about your mother in the past tense. What happened?*

But he leaned back and closed his eyes, lifting his face to the sun, and gradually, she realized he wasn't going to ask.

Relief washed through her, and she blew out a silent, shaky breath, filled with gratitude that he recognized she didn't want to talk, and was willing to let it pass.

She watched a huge butterfly flap slowly through the flowers. "Is that a Red Admiral?"

"Yes. Maori call them *kahukura*. It means 'red cloak.'"

"I like that."

"Will you miss England if you stay here?" he asked.

"I don't think so. I had one or two friends but no huge social group as I didn't get out much, sad as that sounds. No partner. The island I come from is very insular—everyone knows everyone else's business—and I'll be glad to get away from that. The idea of coming here, where nobody knows me or my past, is so exciting, I can't tell you."

"Have you applied for residency?"

She shook her head. "We're here on a working holiday visa, which means we can work for up to twelve months and extend for another three. But the plan is really to take a few days to see if we want to give it a go, and if we do, a few months to make sure, and then if all goes well, apply for full residency. With our father having been a Kiwi, it shouldn't be a problem. I suppose that even if the vineyard doesn't work out, technically we could still stay and just live and work elsewhere, but I don't know that we would do that. We came here to make the vineyard work. If we don't have that… I don't know what we're going to do."

Her throat tightened, and she stopped speaking. She felt embarrassed that she'd said too much, even though she hadn't told him the worst of it. She barely knew the guy. She believed in his desire to right his father's wrongs, but he was still a MacDonald, and all three Cartwright girls had been burned for trusting when they should have been more cautious.

But he just said, "All right. You said that Sandi and Ginger are going to take the day to investigate their neck of the woods. You've had a look around the vineyard and the winery. Let's grab some lunch, and then how about we take another shot at the house?"

"Sure." The idea of some physical work appealed to her. She'd help him clear out the rooms and do some cleaning—it never failed to make her feel better. When her body was busy, it left her mind free to work on the problem. Maybe then, it would become clear to her what they should do.

So they joined the girls and took a seat in the restaurant, and Mac ordered them a couple of platters. They weren't very good, and Fred exchanged a glance with Ginger, knowing her sister was busy drawing up menus in her head and would already have quizzed the kitchen staff on sourcing local food, including fresh fish and seafood from the bay.

For the first time, Mac treated them to a glass of wine with their meal. Sandi wanted white, so he recommended the vineyard's Chardonnay. He told them it had a good oak and citrus balance, with a refreshing finish, and would go nicely with the Brie cheese. And for the rest of them he chose a Syrah, with its plum and savory black pepper flavors, which he said went well with the Cheddar and Gouda cheeses.

Fred tried both wines as she ate, pleasantly surprised by how nice they were, and a little excited about the fact that they were made from grapes growing in their own vineyard.

She listened to Ginger and Sandi chat away about the B&B and the restaurant as she ate, hoping their enthusiasm was contagious and that it would encourage her to find an answer to her side of the problem. But it was difficult to find a way out of the maze. The vineyard needed serious money spent on it. She had no money, and no way to get any. Maybe if she got residency, she'd be able to take out a mortgage? She'd have to investigate whether she'd be able to pay herself enough of a wage to meet the payments. She hadn't expected to just arrive and have the money rolling in, but the last thing she wanted was to get knee-deep in debt.

After lunch, when Ginger and Sandi returned to their cataloguing and note-taking, Fred went with Mac and Scully back to the house, where they spent the afternoon finishing off the tidying of the second bedroom. She'd hoped maybe to find some more of her father's effects, but it all turned out to be rubbish—torn bits of carpet, old magazines, empty wine bottles, bits of an old dog kennel, parts of a car engine, broken mugs… you name it, she found it in there.

Most of it, she presumed, was James's junk. How much of this stuff had been her father's? It was odd to think this had been Harry's place for so many years, and his parents' before that. She knew that her paternal grandparents were both dead, and Harry had been an only child, but presumably she had distant relatives across New Zealand. She'd have to research one day and see if she could contact some.

By six o'clock, the room was empty of rubbish, vacuumed, and cleaned. Fred was tired, too tired to go down into the bay to eat, but hungry nevertheless, so Mac volunteered to drive out and fetch a takeaway. He returned with several bags from the Indian restaurant, and the four of them sat in the dining room in the house to eat, dipping pieces of poppadum into the tiny pots of raita and mango chutney, and scooping the hot and spicy curries up with chunks of naan bread.

Fred sipped from the glass of Sauvignon Blanc that Mac had recommended to go with her butter chicken. She was nowhere near as good as he was at picking out the notes of a wine, but even she could taste the gooseberries, with a hint of grapefruit.

She cast the occasional glance at him as she ate. He'd been an interesting companion while they'd worked that afternoon. It had grown warm in the house, and at one point he'd stripped to the waist, revealing a toned, tanned body with impressive muscles that had glowed in the afternoon sun. He had an interesting tattoo—not the full upper arm and shoulder she'd seen on the pictures of some of the All Blacks rugby players, but a ring around his upper arm, in the shape of stylized waves. Did they represent the Pacific? She was too shy to ask, but found her gaze drawn to it repeatedly.

She'd tried to keep her eyes averted, but it hadn't been easy. He was a fine specimen of a man, and she liked his attitude that anything could be sorted providing you put enough hard work into it.

He talked too, sometimes, telling her about his childhood in Russell, about fishing off the pier, going out into the Bay of Islands and diving for kingfish and mussels. He talked about friends, but never mentioned a sibling, so she thought he was probably an only child. He mentioned his mother several times, speaking about her in a fond, teasing tone that made Fred want to meet her.

But he never mentioned his father. Fred didn't think it was just because of what James MacDonald had done to the estate. It went deeper than that, she was sure, some simmering resentment that sent roots way back into his past. One day, she'd ask him about it. If he stayed. He'd looked surprised that morning when she'd told him she hoped he'd play a part in getting the vineyard back on its feet. Did he already have other plans? Had he been applying for jobs elsewhere in the country?

Did he have a girl that he was thinking about?

It was none of her business, Fred told herself. She had to keep her head clear. The vineyard had to come first, and even though she'd spent all day going over ideas in her head, trying to work out where they could cut corners without sacrificing the quality of the wine, she was no nearer to coming to a conclusion, and making a success of the place seemed as much of a distant dream as ever.

Chapter Nine

"So how did your research go into the B&B and restaurant?" Mac asked Ginger and Sandi while they all tucked into their curries.

"Good," Ginger mumbled through a mouthful of rice and naan. "There's huge potential here. The kitchen's not in bad nick—some of the equipment could do with replacing, but it's not essential. The biggest issue is the menu, and the sourcing of local produce. And I'd love to get trained waiters and waitresses rather than local teens who don't know a dessert spoon from a soup spoon, or at least train the local teens to the proper standard. And of course, the restaurant itself needs bringing into the twenty-first century. Not in its look—I love the flagstones and the kauri wood bar—but fresh paint, new tables and chairs, new cutlery and crockery, that kind of stuff. It all costs money, though."

"What *has* to be done?" Fred asked her. "As opposed to what you'd like to do."

"None of it *has* to be done, I guess. But I'm not sure I'm prepared to settle for mediocre." Ginger frowned and poked at a piece of chicken with her fork. Mac understood what she meant. There was no point in doing anything by halves. If she couldn't bring the restaurant up to the standards she'd been hoping, she'd be better off returning to the UK and taking over an already-performing restaurant.

"What about the B&B?" Fred asked her other sister.

"Much the same," Sandi said. "There's plenty I'd like to do. New linen and curtains, a complete re-decoration throughout, a fresh look for the dining room, a new washing machine and tumble dryer for the laundry. Plus of course the pool could do with a new fence, and the garden needs quite a bit of work done to it. Doesn't *have* to be done. But if we don't do it, we're starting off half cock, so to speak."

Mac watched Fred lay her fork on the plate and push it away, her appetite clearly disappearing. "Yeah," she said, somewhat listlessly. "It's a similar story with the vineyard, and of course, as we said, if the vineyard is failing, there's little point in getting everything else sorted."

"Don't lose heart." Sandi rested a hand on Fred's. "Not yet. Give us another day to think about it. I'm not done yet and neither is Ginger. We're going to come up with a series of plans—what absolutely must be done, what's next, what's not so important, that kind of thing. Then we'll have a better idea of cost."

"All right." Fred pushed away from the table. "I might go for a walk. Don't do the washing up—I'll tackle it when I get back."

They watched her go, and then Ginger and Sandi looked at Mac.

"She really wants this," Ginger said.

"Yeah." Mac started to gather together the foil containers. "I can see that."

"She's had a tough time, that's all," Sandi said, "we all have, actually, and we were hoping that this would be the answer, you know? I don't mean to guilt you, I'm just saying it like it is."

"I understand. Fred explained that things have been difficult for you."

As one, their eyebrows rose.

"Really?" Ginger said.

"Yeah." He frowned at their surprise.

Sandi exchanged a glance with her sister. "Only… she never talks to anyone. We've never been able to get her to see a counsellor, and even her friends, such as they are, don't know the full story."

"I'm not sure I know the full story," he admitted, "but she told me about your mum's illness, and that she'd burned Harry's letters to you, and hidden the ones that Fred wrote him."

"Wow, you must be something," Ginger said, "to get her talking."

"Not really." He shifted in his chair and concentrated on stacking the plates. "We shared a moment, I guess." He finished tidying, then leaned back in his chair. "I get the feeling she's not told me everything."

The girls exchanged a glance. "If Fred didn't want to tell you, it's not our place to say," Sandi said quietly.

Disappointed, he gave a reluctant nod. "You're a long way from home, and you had quite a shock yesterday when you discovered the full extent of what my father had done. I'm aware you all set your hearts on the place, and it's been a disappointment for you."

Ginger scratched at a mark on the table. "A bit."

"We did all have high hopes that this would be the answer to what was missing from our lives." Sandi leaned forward, catching his eye. "And we've all had it hard, there's no doubt about it. But I think it's been hardest on Fred."

Harder than losing your partner, and then discovering he'd been married the whole time? Or having your ex accuse you of stealing from your company and getting you sacked? Mac stared at her, puzzled. "Do you think so?"

Both girls nodded. "She's the definition of the word stoic," Sandi said. "She looked after our mother for years, and never complained. Did she tell you that she didn't go to university but went out to work so that we could both go?"

"No," he admitted.

"She gave up so much for us. I feel ashamed now." Sandi's cheeks flushed red. "I just didn't realize at the time. It must have been so hard for her. She missed out on the chance to have a career."

"She wanted to be a nurse," Ginger added.

"Really?" Mac could see her in the role, patient and kind. He tried not to dwell on the uniform.

"She never really had the chance to have a decent run at a relationship either," Sandi said. "She went out with guys occasionally, but they never lasted very long, probably because they weren't prepared to play second-best to our mother. But she never complained. She gave Mum everything, and then she found out Mum had been lying to us the whole time. It was such a betrayal, especially for Fred, because she can remember Dad. But all three of us missed out on a chance to know our father because of our mother." Sandi's voice was bitter. Ginger said nothing, just stared mutely at her hands.

"You've all been through a lot," Mac said gently. "And I'm glad you came to the bay. We'll do our best to work something out. Fred wants to give it another day for you to think about the B&B and restaurant, and for us to try to come up with a plan. So take your time, and try not to worry."

"Yes, Dad," Ginger said.

He gave her a wry look. "I'm just trying to help."

Her expression softened. "I know."

"I'm going to find Fred." He rose and tucked his chair under the table.

"We'll clean up," Sandi said. "Take your time."

Ginger nudged her with her elbow. Sandi nudged her back.

Mac pretended not to have noticed. "Okay, thanks."

He headed out and crossed the garden, Scully at his heels, looking toward the vineyard to see if he could spot Fred. He thought about how her sisters had nudged each other. They thought that Fred liked him. Well, he liked her too, so that was something. When he remembered how he'd dreaded the girls arriving—had thought there would be screaming and tears and cursing—he couldn't have wished for a better outcome. The sisters were lovely, Fred especially, and their attitude toward him had been much more than he deserved.

The vineyard glowed in the setting sun, the grapes plump and rich and ready for harvesting, which would begin in the next week or two. The weather had been perfect, dry and warm with just the right amount of rain, so at least it should be a decent vintage.

As he rounded the buildings, he saw her, walking away from him along the edge of the vineyard on the Pacific side. He jogged down to catch her up, Scully bouncing beside him, not considering until he neared her that she might want to be alone.

"Hey," he said, slowing down when he reached her.

She looked up at him, eyebrows rising. "Hi."

"I wondered whether you wanted company, then realized when I got here that you probably didn't. You want me to leave you to it?"

She smiled. "No, that's okay. I just wanted to stretch my legs."

He fell into step with her, and they walked in silence for a while, the only sound coming from the German Shepherd as she snuffled amongst the leaves. The ocean glowed a deep russet with gold-topped waves.

"It's so beautiful here," Fred said eventually. She took a sip from a glass, and he saw then that she'd brought her wine with her.

"I think so."

"In his letter, Dad said something about the bay being his place to stand."

"*Turangawaewae?*"

"That's the word—I didn't realize you pronounced it like that. *Too-ranga-why-why*," she repeated. "I didn't really understand what he meant before, but I feel it here, Mac. I feel as if I belong here. I know it's probably dramatic and pretentious considering we only set foot here yesterday, but..."

"It's not," he said quietly. "It runs in the blood, resides in the heart. Have you read or seen *Gone with the Wind*? 'The land is the only thing in the world worth working for, worth fighting for, worth dying for, because it's the only thing that lasts.' Margaret Mitchell understood. People and money and success and failure come and go, but the land is always there."

Fred's eyes glistened, and she gave a small laugh and rubbed her nose. "You're an old romantic at heart, aren't you?"

"Hey, less of the old."

She grinned. "How old are you?"

"Thirty-two. You?"

"Thirty in a few months. The big three-oh." She pulled a face.

"It's not so bad. Think of it as a celebration. In the medieval period, you'd probably be dead by now, after having had fifteen children. You're thirty! You made it!"

She laughed. "Thanks. I think."

They walked a little farther in silence.

"So…" he said eventually. "You're not leaving anyone behind in the U.K.?"

She chewed her bottom lip. "No."

"I'm surprised."

She wrinkled her nose. "That's sweet of you. But men weren't exactly climbing over each other to get to me. Not that I wanted them to. I'm going to be a crazy cat lady. An old maid, crocheting and making jam until I pop my clogs."

"Pop your clogs? I haven't heard that one."

"Until I snuff it. Give up the ghost. Kick the bucket. Push up daisies."

"Shuffle off the mortal coil," he said.

"Sleep with the fishes."

"Do not pass go, do not collect two-hundred dollars," he said.

"Check into the horizontal Hilton," Fred finished, and they both laughed.

"I always thought I wanted to be buried here," Mac said. "In the middle of the vines."

"It would give a nice earthy touch to the Chardonnay."

"Ha! Yeah."

She hesitated. "Where's my father…"

"He was cremated, as per his wishes, and his ashes were scattered at the local crematorium. There's a plaque there. I'll take you all to see it, if you like."

She nodded, but didn't say anything.

They turned the corner at the bottom of the vineyard and started heading back up the hill.

"I like that you don't mind talking about dying," she said. "I know that sounds odd, but I've never met anyone who has the same… I dunno, pragmatic view, I suppose, as me."

He shrugged. "Maybe it's spending so much time outdoors. Working with the vines, it gives you a cyclical view of life. Seeds are planted, they grow, bear fruit, then they die, but death is just a big sleep in nature, isn't it? A kind of hibernation. That's how I like to think of it, anyway." He gestured at the vineyard. "Harry's still here, somewhere, watching you now. I bet he's thrilled to see you here."

"Maybe. It's a nice thought." She blew out a long breath, then finished off her glass of wine. "Life's so short, isn't it? It's easy to tiptoe through it, trying not to make waves. I've spent my life being a good girl, doing what I thought was right, and look where it got me. I'm tired of it, Mac. Of doing what other people want me to do. I want to be selfish, for a change. Not to worry about what people are thinking of me."

"Sounds fair to me."

She turned to him. "I want to put my dreams first. I don't know how yet, but I'm determined to make this work, even if I have to put in twelve hours, seven days a week."

It wouldn't be enough, but he loved the way her eyes were blazing, filled with a light that he was certain hadn't been there for a long time. "Then we'll do it."

"I mean it. I'm not going without a fight. Ginger, Sandi, and I—we've gone through too much, suffered enough. Other people have made our lives a misery, and we're all tired of it. If we want happiness, we're going to have to find it ourselves. Nobody's going to hand it to us on a plate."

None of the girls would find it easy to trust again. It made him sad, but he could understand why they felt like that. Once again, he felt a flare of anger toward his father, who had selfishly ridden roughshod over these girls' lives, not thinking about what his destructive behavior was doing to their inheritance, to their spirit, or indeed, to his own son. Fred was right—you made your own happiness in life, and he admired the girls for recognizing that and acting on it.

"Just tell me what you want me to do," he said, "and I'll do my best to help."

She gave a firm nod and looked across the vineyard. Her gaze turned briefly wistful, and he thought she might be thinking of her father, and his own words about Harry's spirit watching over her. Then he saw her chin lift, and knew determination was setting in.

"Let's go back to the house," she said. "There's something I want to do, and you're the man to do it."

Chapter Ten

"A wine tasting?" Sandi grinned. "Now you're talking."

They'd returned to the house, and Fred had announced her suggestion. Ginger and Sandi had just finished washing the dishes, and their eyes lit up.

"What do you think?" Fred asked Mac.

"Now?" he said.

"I want to sample the merchandise." She lifted her gaze to his and held it.

The corners of his lips curved up. "Whatever the customer wants."

Her heart banged against her ribs. She mustn't flirt with him. But it was impossible not to. The guy was so… it was hard to put it into words. He was gorgeous, but that wasn't the only reason she liked him so much. She'd previously compared him to Tangaroa, the Maori sea god, because of his blue eyes, but now she found herself thinking of him more as a nature deity, like Herne the Hunter or the Green Man. He'd said things about the land and nature that made her shiver. Nobody had ever come close to expressing the way she felt about life. He was a complete stranger, and yet oddly, in the one day since she'd known him, she felt as if he understood her more than her mother, her sisters, or any of her friends had ever done.

"Why don't we go back to the B&B," he said. "That way, when we're done you can just roll down the corridor straight to bed."

"Sounds like a great idea," Ginger replied.

"I thought the idea of wine tasting was to spit it out," Sandi commented.

"It's entirely up to you whether you want to spit or swallow," he said.

Ginger snorted and Sandi laughed. Fred raised her eyebrows.

Mac ran a hand through his hair. "You won't believe me, but actually I was referring to the wine." When Fred grinned, he gave a rueful smile and just rolled his eyes. "Technically, the true sommelier won't swallow or else he or she will get drunk every time they go to work. But tonight? I think you've earned the right to get a bit tipsy. Come on."

They all went over to the B&B, and Mac told them to sit in the dining room while he fetched the bottles. Scully stayed with them, as if she'd decided she was one of the girls now.

"That was deliciously cute," Ginger said when he'd left. "He's quite gorgeous when he's not being all dark and broody."

"He's devastated by what his father did." Fred retrieved four wine glasses from the cabinet, placed them on the table, and sat. "Absolutely gutted, and determined to make it up to us."

"We mustn't let that go to waste," Ginger said.

"Ginger," Sandi scolded. "I don't care what we've both been through—we don't take advantage of other people like that."

"Oh, keep your knickers on. I just meant that if he's offering help, we'd be stupid to ignore it."

"I've already told him that I'm hoping he'll stick around to advise us," Fred told them. "I know all three of us find it difficult to trust people now, but let's face it—if we decide we want to make a go of it here, we're going to need all the help we can get."

"Have you made up your mind yet?" Sandi glanced at the door to make sure Mac hadn't yet returned.

Fred met her gaze. "Have you?"

Sandi shrugged. When they looked at Ginger, she shrugged, too. They all gave low chuckles.

"Tomorrow," Fred promised. "We'll sit down at the end of the day, cards on the table, and go through everything."

They all nodded.

"Do you think Mac's a typical Kiwi guy?" Ginger asked.

"What do you mean?"

"I wonder if they're all like him. If so… I think we're going to have some fun while we're here."

Fred opened her mouth to reply, but he walked back in at that moment, so she shut it again.

He was carrying five bottles, and as he set them on the table, Fred saw that he'd brought one of each of the types of grapes they grew at the bay—Chardonnay, Merlot, Syrah, Pinot Gris, and Chambourcin.

He also had a box of chocolates from an intriguingly named shop called *Treats to Tempt You*, which he laid alongside the bottles. "Help yourself," he said, taking a seat opposite Fred.

"You are absolutely divine." Sandi opened the box, pulled one out, and popped it in her mouth.

"Sandi's a chocoholic," Fred explained.

"And you're not?" He pointed the box at her.

She shrugged and chose a caramel creme. "Is there a woman in the world who isn't?"

He smiled and turned the bottles so the labels faced them. "Where do you want to start?"

"We're in your hands," Sandi said. "You choose."

"Okay." He unscrewed the top from the bottle of Merlot. "This is our crowd pleaser. It has tones of chocolate and cherry, so it'll go well with the truffles." He poured a small amount into each glass.

"What's the difference between a Merlot and a Cabernet Sauvignon?" Fred pulled the nearest glass toward her. She took a deep inhale of the wine and immediately smelled the cherries he'd talked about.

"I brought a color chart." Mac laid it on the table before them. It featured photos of six glasses of wine, all reds. He tapped the first. "The color is caused by how long the grape skins are allowed to soak in the wine. With a Cab Sav, you can see the color is deeper and richer than the Merlot. The Cab Savs have more tannin, which is that dry sensation in the mouth."

Fred took a sip. "Mmm. That's a nice wine."

"Here's a story for you," he said. "Both the Cab Sav and Merlot were born in Bordeaux, in France, on either side of the Gironde river. The left bank was better suited for Cabernet, the right for Merlot. So you can also ask for a left or right bank Bordeaux in a wine shop. That'll score you some points."

"I love stories like that," Ginger said.

Mac ran his tongue across his top lip. "Oh, I've plenty more where that came from. Come on, drink up. Let's compare it to the Syrah."

Fred finished her Merlot, trying to suppress the shiver that had run through her when he'd licked his lip. Now he knew they weren't going to be angry with him, he was starting to relax, and she was beginning to realize there was a much more playful guy beneath the reserved front he'd been projecting.

They compared the spicy Syrah they'd had with dinner to the Merlot, and then tried the Chambourcin.

"It's a hybrid grape," Mac explained, "which a lot of winemakers don't like because they prefer 'pure' wine. But it's resistant to disease, and it's good for blending—in Australia they use it to add color and depth to Shiraz, for example. Can you taste the black cherry and plum?"

"Um…" Fred sipped it again. "Sort of."

"I can taste fruit," Ginger said.

Mac rolled his eyes. "Well if you're going to work on a vineyard, you'll have to do better than that. Drink up. Time to try the whites."

By now, Fred was feeling nicely relaxed, as if she'd been all sharp corners and angles, and someone had come along with sandpaper and filed them off. She had another chocolate while Mac took the glasses off to rinse them, then came back and refilled them from the bottle of Chardonnay.

"Here's a joke for you," Mac said as he poured. "A convent's mother superior called all her nuns together to share some troubling news. She said, 'My dear sisters, we've found a case of Gonorrhea in the convent.' 'Thank the Lord,' one of the nuns said. 'I was getting sick of Chardonnay.'"

Sandi coughed into her glass, and Ginger and Fred burst out laughing.

"I love it," Fred said. "I'm going to write that down."

Mac winked at her and handed her a glass. She took it, feeling a glow inside that she wasn't entirely sure was due to the wine.

"This is aged for eight months in oak barrels," he said. "It smells of peaches and tastes of creamy butterscotch."

"Mmm," Ginger said. "It's lovely."

"I'm not normally a big Chardonnay fan," Fred said, "but it is nice."

Mac finished off his glass. "Chardonnay's a bit of a Marmite wine. People either tend to love it or hate it. I think ours is nicer than the more acidic Chardonnays. You can taste our sub-tropical climate in this wine, I think—it's the one I'm most proud of."

Fred could see what he meant—she could certainly taste the peach and citrus notes in it. The lemon reminded her of Mac, with his fresh lemony scent. But then everything was making her think of Mac at the moment.

There was something magical about the evening—she could feel it unfurling, spreading through the room. The evening sunlight slanted across the table in bars of orange-gold, and her senses were filled with the smell and taste of chocolate and fruit, rich, late-summer tastes that she thought would always make her think of laughter and a full belly, and give a pleasant drowsiness to her eyelids.

It was lovely to see Sandi with her feet up on a chair and her head propped on a hand, laughing as she listened to Mac telling another story about someone who'd visited the vineyard. Sandi hadn't laughed much at all lately. And Ginger—who had become harder and much more defensive since she'd been fired and accused of stealing—looked as if she'd finally let her guard down for a while.

And the cause of all this was the man standing before them, who had switched on his entertaining role, and appeared to be thoroughly enjoying himself as he related facts about the wine and teased the girls with his inimitable wit.

He was now unscrewing the bottle of Pinot Gris. "Apparently, they've developed a new hybrid grape," he said. "It acts as an anti-diuretic, and it's supposed to reduce the number of times you have to go to the bathroom in the night."

Ginger frowned. "What's it called?"

"Pinot More."

Fred snorted and held out her glass for him to splash some into. "You have this performance off pat, don't you?"

"Damn straight. Did you know that in the sixteenth century Martin Luther said, 'Beer is made by men, wine by God'?"

"And Pope John XXIII said, 'Men are like wine—some turn to vinegar, but the best improve with age.'"

He grinned. "Which one am I?"

"I'll let you know when I get to know you better."

He chuckled and gestured at her glass. "Tell me what you think of that."

She inhaled tropical fruit, melon, and mango, and when she sipped it, the wine tasted rich and almost oily. "It's nice," she said. "Different. I really like it."

"So." He gestured to the bottles before him. "What's your favorite?"

"I like the Pinot Gris," Sandi said. "It's lovely."

"The Cabernet for me," Ginger replied. "I prefer a red."

"So do I normally." Fred considered the bottles, and her gaze rested on the Chardonnay. She thought about its lemony scent, and how it had reminded her of Mac. "I'm going to surprise myself and choose this," she said, tapping the bottle.

She met his gaze and felt an inner glow as his smile spread slowly. He was pleased with her choice. It shouldn't matter, but for some reason it did.

"So, Chardonnay for you." He poured some more into her glass, then topped up the other girls' glasses with their favorites. After pouring himself some of the Chardonnay, he said, "If I may suggest a toast… To Blue Penguin Bay."

"To Blue Penguin Bay," Fred and her sisters repeated, and they all sipped their wine.

"I'm glad we came," Sandi said, "whatever happens now."

"Me too," Ginger added, which pleased Fred. At least they weren't all regretting coming here.

"Mac said he'd take us to the crematorium, where Dad has a plaque," she told them. "If you want to go."

They both nodded. "It's funny to think of him living here," Sandi said. "I mean, that this was his land. That it's our land."

Fred glanced at Mac, but he just smiled.

"I hope you don't feel that we took it away from you," she said to him.

"I don't." He reached for the bottle and poured some more Chardonnay into both their glasses. "Part of me knew I was only here on borrowed time. It was a nice fantasy, but life generally doesn't gift you things like that."

"So…" Ginger stared pointedly at his empty hand. "You're not married, then?"

"Nope." He sipped his wine. He didn't smile, but something told Fred that he was amused by her direct question.

"And not living with anyone?" Ginger persisted. Fred wanted to tell her to stop being so nosy, but she couldn't get the words out because she really wanted to know.

"Nope." He sighed. "I haven't dated for a while. There was a girl, some time ago, when I was in Blenheim, but it didn't work out." He met Fred's gaze briefly, then dropped it back to his glass.

"So," she said, pulling the bottle toward her. "None of us have anyone to nag us for coming home drunk. Excellent!"

They all laughed and refilled their glasses, and for the next hour or so, as the sun sank into the west, they finally let themselves go. They ate all the chocolates and sent Mac out to the kitchen to find some crackers and cheese, then ate those while they continued to talk, until the wine levels dropped in the bottles and they couldn't drink any more.

Sandi yawned and stretched, and said, "I know it's not late, but I really ought to go to bed."

"Lightweight," Ginger accused, although she was practically asleep on the table. "Yeah, me too."

"Go on," Fred told them, "you go in. I'll take the glasses to the kitchen, then I'll join you."

The two of them stumbled off. In the background came the sound of someone crashing into something, and then they both giggled.

Fred met Mac's gaze, and they both smiled. "That did them the world of good," Fred said softly. "Thank you."

"You all looked like you needed to relax." He sighed. "It was good for me too."

"I'm glad. You've obviously had a tough time, as well."

Her gaze lingered on him. He now had a decent five o'clock shadow, and his eyes were half lidded, although he wasn't slurring his words or anything. Fred had drunk more than she would normally limit herself to, and she hoped she wasn't going to make a fool of herself. Not that she cared anymore. Something about Mac made her feel as if she could throw off all the cares and worries that had plagued her since… well, forever. He didn't seem bothered by the social constraints that had been part of her life in the U.K., like wearing the newest fashions or driving the correct car to project the right image. He drove what he called a 'ute', which turned out to be a utility vehicle or a huge, battered pickup truck, and clearly designer clothing played no part in his life.

His blue eyes had darkened, like the sea itself as the sun set, and for once he didn't look away when she met his gaze. A small smile appeared on his lips, but he continued to watch her, sitting back in his chair, turning his wine glass around by the stem.

"What are you looking at?" She meant it to sound sassy, but it came out kind of breathless and hopeful.

"Your hair," he said, surprising her. "I've never seen hair as long as yours in real life. It's beautiful."

His compliment threw her. He didn't seem like the kind of guy who tossed them around willy nilly, and although he'd called her beautiful before they'd gotten in the car, she was sure he hadn't meant her to hear it.

"Oh," she said. "Thank you."

He gave a small shrug, and smiled again.

Bemused, because she didn't get compliments very often, and certainly not from gorgeous men, she gathered together the wine glasses, stood, then laughed as the world tilted and the glasses clattered together.

"Careful." He rose too and collected the bottles. "Come on, you can lean on me if you like."

"You're drunk too," she scolded as they walked back into the kitchen.

"I'm mellow," he corrected, "not drunk."

"Mellow." She liked the description. It seemed to capture the whole of New Zealand.

He put the wine bottles in the recycling bin, and she placed the glasses carefully by the sink, determining it would be best to wash them up the next morning.

"It's warm tonight," she said, although it was probably the alcohol that gave her a glow in her cheeks.

"Want to catch some fresh air?" He gestured at the door.

"Sure." Trying to ignore the hammer of her heart, she let him open it for her, and went out into the fresh autumn air.

Chapter Eleven

The breeze brushed light fingers through Mac's hair as they walked through the garden. Scully ran around sniffing, tail up, and he almost felt like joining her. It was a beautiful evening, and as they exited through the gate and walked along the edge of the vineyard, Blue Penguin Bay lay beneath them, bathed in glorious colors, like a bowl of ripe fruit, oranges and strawberries and the deep purples and blues of grapes.

"Oh," Fred whispered, coming to a stop as she observed the view.

Mac stopped too, but turned his gaze instead to her, finding her as beautiful—if not more so—than the sunset. The rays had turned her hair to copper, and her skin was a pretty blush pink, although that could also have been the wine. She'd kept up with him, but although she'd relaxed and the dimples in her cheeks had appeared more frequently, she was steady on her feet and obviously knew her limits, which he admired.

Her nose was straight, tip-tilted a little at the end, and her lips were neither too wide nor too full, just right. She wasn't stunningly beautiful, but she had a quality he liked, a classy poise that made her stand out from most of the other women he'd met. She was intelligent, but she didn't make him feel stupid. Would she stay? He found himself crossing his fingers, hoping she would.

Her lashes fluttered down—she knew he was watching her. She didn't look up at him, though. She continued walking, and he fell into step beside her.

They shouldn't go too far at this time of night—the insects would be biting, and he wasn't sure if she'd thought to put on insect repellent. He still got bitten, but the bites no longer bothered him. Tourists frequently suffered, though, their rich blood tasty offerings for the mosquito and sandfly.

But he didn't want the evening to end, so he kept silent, breathing in the autumnal air.

"Harvest soon?" she asked. The sunset colors were fading, the moon—three-quarters full—now providing most of the light, and her face was half in shadow.

"Yep. It'll be a busy few weeks." It was no good—he was going to have to ask. "Do you think you'll be here for it?"

She glanced up at him. "I'm not sure yet. We're going to talk about it tomorrow."

"You don't have a gut feeling?"

She returned her gaze to the grass. "I want to stay. I feel I belong here. I certainly don't feel I belong in the U.K. anymore. But financially, I'm still not sure what to do. I don't want to sink the vineyard just because I'm too stubborn to let it go. I've no doubt the four of us could keep it ticking over for a while, but that's not good enough, is it? It deserves better than that."

The four of us. She'd included him in her plans. A warm glow spread through him.

She stopped again at the corner of the vineyard and looked down at the bay. "I'm ready for a new life, Mac. I want to begin again. This is my chance to have a real job, a career, something I can throw myself into, you know? I've so enjoyed researching about winemaking. I know I have a huge amount to learn—I'm not saying I believe I can just walk in and do what you do right off the bat."

"Of course not," he said, "that's why you have an estate manager. He or she brings the experience, and you work together. It's no different than what Harry did—he loved the vineyard, but he left the day-to-day running of it to other people, including my father. They seemed to work well together, which I guess is why it was such a shock when Dad did what he did."

Fred turned away from the view of the Pacific, and they began to walk back to the buildings. "Why did your dad do it, do you think?"

"We'll never know. I suspect it was a spur of the moment decision. He knew Harry wasn't in contact with his children. He saw an opportunity, and he took it. And then afterward, the guilt weighed so heavily on him that it sent him mad." Mac's jaw tightened. That was the best-case scenario. The worst was that his father had planned all along to take over, which would make him far more mean and cut-throat than Mac had given him credit for. He didn't want to remember his father like that, if only because he feared some of that mean nature might have transferred to himself.

"You're not like him," Fred said, as if reading his mind. "Not that I've seen, anyway. Don't worry."

"What made you think it worries me?"

"Because I'm the same. You don't think I fear that I'm going to discover one day that I'm bipolar? That I have the same tendency to self-destruct as my mother?"

"You don't seem like that at all."

"No." She tilted her face up to the moon and closed her eyes briefly. "Not so far, anyway. I thank our lucky stars every day that all three of us seem to have escaped that curse, but of course you never know—it could be lurking in the genes, ready to pounce at any time."

"You don't seem high maintenance," he said. "In fact, you seem very easy. Uh… I don't mean…"

She laughed and bumped shoulders with him. "Well, cheers."

"This is why I don't talk to people."

"Aw. You don't socialize much?"

"Hardly at all. I have a couple of mates in the bay, and we go fishing occasionally, but that's about it."

"And there's no girl here trying to lure you like a siren?" Her teasing tone belied her curious look.

"No. Not even close."

The evening breeze played with her hair, making it look as if it had a life of its own, as if it could reach out and wrap around him, pull him close. Once or twice it brushed his arm, and the soft touch made him shiver.

For a long time now, he'd kept his feelings and desire locked deep inside. He'd been hibernating, he thought, for many years. After breaking up with Claire and leaving Blenheim, he'd backed away from dating, from women completely, and had almost resigned himself to the fact that he was probably going to live the rest of his life alone. It wasn't that she'd broken his heart to the point of no return, more that he'd loved her but they'd grown apart, and it had been hard to admit it was over and that he'd failed to make the relationship work. He hadn't thought he had the energy for romance anymore. He liked sex as much as the next man, but the hoops you had to jump through to establish a relationship seemed out of his reach, and he wasn't the sort of guy who indulged in one-night stands.

Oddly, it had been okay. He'd filled his days with the vineyard, and his nights with reading and studying and watching TV, and he was happy, or content, anyway. He'd honestly thought he could see out his days like that.

And then Fred had turned up.

He looked at her now, at her pale, slender neck that was exposed when her hair lifted, at her blush-filled cheeks, at her soft mouth, and once again the sleeping bear stirred inside him, growled, raised its head, and yawned. It was the wine—of course, it was the wine—but his blood felt hot, rushing around his body, warming it, making his heart thunder, making desire rise inside him in a way it hadn't for oh, so long.

He shouldn't say anything or do anything—he should keep his thoughts and hands to himself, because they'd both drunk too much, and the situation was far too volatile to muddy it with any kind of physical complication.

But Fred stopped, and when he turned to face her, he saw something in her expression that only made his heart pound faster.

They were already standing close, but the few inches between them disappeared, although he wasn't sure if she'd moved or if he had. He liked her height—just two or three inches shorter than him—he'd only have to bend his head a little and his lips would touch hers.

She tilted her face up to his, and he looked into her eyes, each of which held a reflection of the moon.

"We shouldn't," she whispered, her lips so close to his. "I know we shouldn't. But… I'm not imagining it, am I? What's happening between us?"

"No." He lifted a hand and slipped a strand of her hair through his fingers. He'd guessed right—it felt like silk ribbon.

"I haven't kissed anyone for…" Her eyebrows rose in surprise. "Oh my God… years."

"Me neither." He continued to wrap the strand of hair around his finger, afraid to let go in case she fled into the night.

"Why now?" she murmured. "I don't understand."

"I guess there's no rhyme or reason to it."

In the distance, a bird hooted, and she turned her head toward it. "An owl?"

"Yes, our only surviving native one. It's called a morepork. Can you hear it say that?"

Her lips curved up. "I can! *More-pork*."

He moved his hand to her face, and touched his thumb to the dimple in her right cheek. "I like these."

Instinctively, she tipped her head to the right to press her cheek into his palm.

"We've had too much to drink," she said.

"I know."

"I wouldn't be doing this if I hadn't."

"I know." He stroked his thumb against her soft skin. "You want me to stop?"

She gave a tiny shake of her head.

He moved forward the last inch, so their bodies touched, and rested his other hand on her hip. He lowered his lips to brush hers.

"You sure?" he murmured.

In answer, she kissed him.

Mac closed his eyes. Her mouth was soft and cool. He pressed his lips to hers gently, half expecting her to pull away once it sank in what they were doing, but she didn't. Instead, she sighed, and then she rested both hands on his chest and leaned into him.

His heart banged on his ribs, but he stayed calm and slipped his arm around her, resting his hand at the base of her spine, holding her tightly. Cupping her head with his other hand, he touched his tongue to her lip, and when her mouth opened, he slid his tongue against hers, deepening the kiss. Fred moaned and splayed her fingers on his chest, and they exchanged a long, sensual, heartfelt kiss, while the morepork hooted softly in the trees, Scully snuffled in the leaves, and the moon turned their skin to silver.

When he finally raised his head, he didn't know if it was the wine or the kiss that made his body feel as if it glowed like a beacon.

"Mmm." She lifted a hand to her lips and moved back a little, and he dropped his arms.

For a long while, they stood there, looking at each other, Fred with her fingers pressed to her mouth.

Eventually, she said, "I'm sorry... I shouldn't have done that."

His heart sank at the thought that she already regretted the kiss, but he forced himself to smile. "It's all right. It was nice. Don't worry about it."

"I should go to bed."

"Yeah. Come on. I'll walk you to the B&B."

In silence, they entered the gate and crossed the garden to the door. He stopped there, and rested a hand on her arm. "I'll see you in the morning."

"Mac…"

He waited. Her brow had furrowed, and she looked as if she was trying to think what to say, and failing.

"It's all right," he said again, and touched her cheek. "It was a shared moment, that's all."

"Yes."

"Don't stress about it. Get some sleep. I'll see you tomorrow."

Lowering his hand, he turned and headed off for the house. Scully waited a second, then trotted after him.

He didn't look back.

*

Normally, if he drank a whole bottle of wine on his own, which wasn't very often, he went to bed, fell asleep, and woke when it was light. Tonight, even though his head felt stuffed with cotton wool and his eyes were heavy, he couldn't get to sleep. He lay awake until the sky was completely dark and filled with stars, and all the while, his mind was full of Winifred Cartwright, and her gentle kiss.

Chapter Twelve

The next morning, Fred walked into the dining room, somewhat bleary eyed, to find the table laid with bowls and spoons and several kinds of cereal, a big pitcher of milk, a jug of hot coffee, and a note.

Morning, it read

I'll be in the barrel hall—Fred, can you come and see me when you've eaten? Mac.

Concise and to the point, she thought, sliding into a seat before placing her head in her hands and closing her eyes.

She couldn't believe she'd kissed him. Jeez. How drunk had she been? Normally, she wasn't the sort of person to do stupid things after a few glasses of wine—she'd never been one of those people who couldn't remember what they'd done.

But she'd kissed him. She'd kissed him! It wasn't even as if she could blame him for grabbing her and giving her no choice in the matter. It had happened slowly, like the rising of the moon, and in a way that had caught her in a spell, until it had seemed as if there was no other way the evening could end.

Her mind kept playing back the way he'd stroked her hair, then brushed her cheek, and how he'd slid his other hand around her waist and pulled her toward him with just the right amount of pressure to be enticingly demanding without being forceful.

But it was a mistake to have given in to the desire that had sparked between them. She'd been lonely, and he'd been convenient, that was all.

She sat back in her chair and bit her lip. That wasn't fair. It implied she'd have kissed any guy who happened to be walking by her side last night, and that wasn't true at all. There was definitely something between them, a simmering attraction she'd kept behind bars like a bird of paradise, and the wine had allowed her to undo the cage and let it fly free for a while.

But there was too much at stake for her to let the bird free forever. She couldn't afford to complicate matters by getting involved with Mac. For a start, she barely knew him, and even though she didn't blame him for what his father had done, and even though she was convinced character flaws weren't handed down from parent to child, nevertheless, he was James MacDonald's son, and she had to be careful.

And not only that, she didn't want to ruin their business relationship. He obviously knew his stuff where winemaking was concerned, and she needed his help if she was going to make a go of the place.

It was a big if, because she still had no idea whether her sisters would want to stay, but until they decided what they were going to do, she had to keep her distance from him.

She tipped some cereal into a bowl, added milk, and ate it while looking out at the garden, thinking about how nice the place would look if given a little TLC. She'd buy a book on New Zealand plants and flowers, and spend some time at the garden center they'd passed on the way out of the bay. In the U.K., her garden had been tiny, just a square patch of lawn with a couple of hanging baskets, but here she'd be able to use her imagination and really make it into something.

If she stayed.

Sighing, she finished her cereal, took the bowl into the kitchen, and washed it up, along with the wine glasses of the night before. Then she returned to the dining room, poured herself a cup of coffee, and headed out. There was no point in trying to put it off— she had to see Mac at some point. Better to get it over with and straighten things out now.

The sky had filled with puffy white clouds and the air had cooled a little. Autumn was definitely on its way. She shivered in her thin shirt, reminding herself to grab her jacket next time, and crossed to the barrel hall.

Scully sat outside the building, and Fred bent to greet her, smiling as the dog licked her hand. Then she pushed open the door and went inside. She saw him immediately, talking to one of the guys who worked on the crushers. Her stomach fluttered, but she forced herself to walk across the tiled floor toward him until she caught his attention.

She didn't miss the way his face lit up when he saw her. She stopped, and he smiled and nodded, then said something to the man he was talking to before walking over to her.

"Come outside," he said before she could speak.

Biting her lip, she followed him out of the door and into the cool air, and they walked away from the buildings, toward the vines, Scully at their side.

"How are you feeling?" he asked.

"Okay, not too bad, surprisingly." She sipped her coffee. His arm was only an inch from hers, and she felt acutely conscious of his bare brown skin. She wanted to reach out and touch it, wanted to stare up into his eyes the way she had the night before, to see that look in them that heated her from her toes to the roots of her hair.

She kept her gaze fixed on the ground though. "Mac, about last night, you know it was a mistake, right?"

"I know that it probably wasn't wise, considering who my father was and what he did."

She glanced at him then. "I'm not saying—"

"I know." He ran a hand through his hair. "I don't want you to worry about it, especially considering that I have an idea I want to put to you."

"Oh?"

"About the vineyard."

"Oh, right." She'd been waiting for this, for him to offer to buy her out. That first night, he'd admitted, *If you were to offer it to me, I'd buy it.* Even though he'd said he'd be happy just being the estate manager, knowing that the girls couldn't afford to revamp the place would surely make him start thinking about buying them out.

"Yeah." He cleared his throat. "I thought of this on day one, but dismissed it as stupid. But I keep thinking about it, so I'm going to say it. Just tell me I'm an idiot if you think it's daft."

Fred frowned. "All right..."

"Marry me," he said.

She stared at him. "What?"

"Marry me. To save the vineyard."

Her heart began to thump hard. "Are you serious?"

"I'm perfectly serious. You'll get access to your inheritance, and it'll go a good way to renewing some of the equipment and getting the vineyard back on its feet."

Her jaw dropped. "Did last night give you this idea?"

"No. Forget about last night, Fred. We were drunk—I know it didn't mean anything. This will be strictly business."

"But..." Her head was whirling. "What would you get out of it?"

"The knowledge that I'll be doing something to put right the terrible things that my father has done."

"By getting yourself hitched?"

His lips quirked up. "It's a small price to pay."

"I... Mac!"

He laughed then. "Forget about the kiss," he said softly. "I'm sorry it happened—well, to be honest, I'm not sorry about the kiss itself because I enjoyed it—but I am sorry that I took advantage of you. I shouldn't have done that."

"You didn't take advantage of me." She bumped her shoulder against him. "Come on, we both know that. It's just... at the moment..."

"Yeah. So, as I said. Forget about the kiss. It'll be strictly business. Nothing personal. It'll just be a contract, our names on a bit of paper. Unfortunately, in New Zealand you have to live apart for two years to get divorced, that's the only thing. If you find your Mr. Right down in the bay, you wouldn't be able to marry him for two years."

Hysterical laughter bubbled from her lips. "I don't think that's going to be a problem."

She stopped at the edge of the vines and turned to face him. His eyes were wide and clear.

"You really mean it," she whispered.

"I do. But you don't have to decide now. Take some time to think about it. Talk it over with the girls. I know Ginger will probably say you're crazy to even think about it." His lips twisted. "But it's a genuine offer."

"Is part of the deal that I keep you on as estate manager?"

He shook his head. "There's no deal, Fred. No caveats or addendums. You know I love it here, and I'd like to stay and work with you to make this place the best vineyard in the Northland. I really think it could be something spectacular. But I understand that you might be wary about keeping me on, and I wouldn't blame you if you decided you'd rather have someone else."

"It's so incredibly generous of you..." She felt bewildered, her brain struggling to comprehend his offer.

"Maybe it'll give you some insight into how bad I feel about what my father did." He shoved his hands into his pockets. "Anyway, I'd better get back to the barrel hall."

"Yes, of course."

"Maybe we'll talk again later?"

"Sure."

"All right." He held her gaze for a moment, then smiled. "I know it must be hard for you to trust anyone at the moment. And I know I kissed you last night. But I mean it when I say this would be strictly business. I'm not trying to force anything onto you. You could draw up whatever pre-nup you liked, put whatever conditions in you wanted. I just want…" He hesitated. "I just want to put things right."

"I know."

He nodded, and turned away, walking back toward the barrel hall. Scully stayed by her side for the moment, looking up at her, and then trotted after him.

She watched him go, her throat tightening. She was lucky to have her sisters, and both Ginger and Sandi would do anything for her. But she'd never had someone on her side like this. Someone who was putting her first, almost above his own needs.

Then she shook her head, frowning. She mustn't look at this with starry eyes. His suggestion wasn't entirely altruistic. There was no such thing as a completely selfless act. He felt bad about what his father had done, and wanted to make himself feel better.

But there were other, easier ways for him to do that, surely? He could have offered to buy her out. But he'd chosen not to do that, because he wanted her to have the vineyard.

Why?

She started to walk slowly back to the house. He'd known Harry Cartwright for a long time, she reminded herself. And he was a Kiwi, with ties to the bay. He loved it here, and he respected the fact that it was her family's land. But even so… Could he really be that noble? Did anyone have principles like that anymore?

Deep in thought, she entered the B&B and went into the dining room, not surprised to see both of her sisters at the breakfast table, tucking into cereal and coffee while they talked.

"Fred!" Sandi gestured at the food with a spoon. "Did you lay this out?"

"No, it was Mac." She sat at the end of the table and refilled her coffee cup.

"So…" Ginger said, obviously continuing a previous conversation, "Amber said her brother supplies all the fish and seafood for Fantails, which is the best restaurant in Paihia, and some of the cafés. He'd be a great contact for my seafood platter. Just imagine—Thai lime and chili prawns, spicy oysters, scallops, the huge green-lipped mussels you get here, fish bites, smoked salmon, and little bowls of dips—garlic aioli, lemon mayonnaise, seafood cocktail. It would be fantastic and would go great with the Pinot Gris, or even the Merlot, anything without heavy tannins."

Fred was impressed that Ginger had thought about pairing the food with the wine. Her sister's eyes were alight with enthusiasm, something she hadn't seen for many months since all the problems with Jack and the restaurant.

"So you still like the idea of staying here?" she asked.

"I do," Ginger said without hesitation. "Of course I do. We talked so much about this place, and it's far better than I imagined. I'd love to stay and make a go of it. At least try. But we've all got to agree."

Fred nodded and turned to her other sister. "What about you?"

"I think it's the most beautiful place I've ever been," Sandi said quietly. "I know I'm going to be biased because it's ours, but I still can't really believe it. We own this estate? That amazes me. If someone were to try to drag me away, I'd hang onto it with my fingertips. I know it's small—four rooms isn't much to play with—but it's more magical, I think, because of that. I'd make the rooms perfect, and work with Ginger to offer amazing breakfasts, and then I'd also work on the pool area and the garden… there's so much we could do. But Ginger's right. We all have to agree, and it's not going to be much fun if we run out of money before we've even gotten started."

"Well, I might have an answer to that," Fred said. She watched her sisters' eyebrows rise and scratched her nose. "Mac's asked me to marry him."

Chapter Thirteen

"Wait," Ginger said. "What?"

Sandi's eyes couldn't have opened any wider. "You're kidding me?"

"Nope." Fred was enjoying the effect of her news now her own shock had worn off a little. "He proposed to me this morning."

"What... how... why..." Ginger couldn't seem to form a sentence.

"Do you... love him?" Sandi looked bewildered.

That made Fred laugh. "No! I've only known him two days. Look, he suggested it as a business deal, to save the vineyard. I'd be able to get my hands on the fifty grand, which would go a good way to starting us off on the right foot. Imagine what we could do with fifty thousand dollars!"

"Yes, but... marriage? It's a bit... extreme," Sandi said.

"It's mental," Ginger added. "I'm guessing you turned him down straightaway?"

Fred turned her mug around in her hands. "No. In fact, I'm considering it."

If Ginger was a cartoon character, her eyes would have fallen out of her head and rolled along the table. "Fred!"

"Look, I was as shocked as you when he first said the words, but he's right, it makes perfect sense." The more Fred thought about it, the more sense it made. "It's just a contract, a signature on a bit of paper."

"No, it's not." Sandi looked suddenly upset. "Since when did we take marriage so lightly?"

"Since our father left all our money tied up in that stupid clause," Fred snapped. "This is the twenty-first century, not the nineteenth. He had no right to place such constrictions on our inheritance, and I'm not going to feel bad for not taking it seriously."

"Would it even work, legally?" Ginger asked. "I mean, would the lawyers accept the marriage if it was so obviously contrived? They will realize it's just a set up to get the money, wouldn't they?"

"Mr. Lyttle joked about it, don't you remember?" Fred referred to their lawyer in the U.K. "He actually said we ought to go out and grab a guy off the street. All they will care about is the signed document, I'm sure of it. I'd check, of course, before we tied the knot, but I'm certain it won't matter. How are they to know we haven't fallen in love in a week and decided to get married, anyway?"

Her two sisters studied her, Sandi worried, Ginger bemused.

"I haven't said yes yet," Fred said softly. It was important to her to get their approval on this. "But it would be a business deal, Mac made that very clear. And in that sense, it's part of the pact we made when we came out here. If either of you is dead set against this, I won't do it. But I want us to discuss it with our heads, not our hearts. This isn't about love or forever—it's a way to access the money, that's all."

She mustn't think about his broad shoulders. About the intriguing tattoo that curled around his arm, how his muscular body gleamed when he worked in the warm sunshine, or how his ocean-blue eyes heated her from the inside out.

She mustn't think about the stolen kiss, the way he'd slipped his arm around her waist to pull her against him. The soft touch of his lips on hers.

"It would be strictly business," she reiterated, to convince herself as much as her sisters.

"Hmm," Ginger said. "I saw the way he looked at you."

"Bullshit." Fred's face burned. "He doesn't look at me any different from the way he looks at you."

Ginger met Sandi's eyes, and they both pursed their lips.

Fred wasn't having that. The kiss had been a thing of the moment, born out of too much wine and the fact that neither of them had kissed anyone for eons. If he'd been out walking with Ginger, he would probably have kissed her.

She ignored the glower of jealousy in her stomach at the thought of Mac kissing either of her sisters.

"Look," she said more gently, leaning forward on the table. "I'm not dissing marriage, I swear. Real marriage is something to be celebrated. It's a way to show commitment, it's a promise that, at that moment, you plan to stay with your partner for the rest of your life. It's a beautiful thing, and maybe one day I'll get around to it. But let's face it, it's not going to happen anytime soon."

"You don't know that," Sandi pointed out. "How do you know that you won't be walking along the bay in six months' time and bump into some gorgeous guy? How's he going to feel when he knows you can't get divorced for another six months?"

"Actually, Mac says you have to have been married two years in New Zealand before you can apply for a divorce…"

Sandi bent and rested her forehead on the table. "This gets worse and worse."

Fred laughed. "Come on, you're making too much of this. It's no different than signing papers when you take out a loan. You sign your life away too, then, don't you? You make a commitment to that company to pay the money, and you pay a penalty if you don't."

"It's hardly the same," Sandi pointed out, sitting up again. "It would feel bizarre to know that you're married to Mac. I don't think I could see it as a business deal."

"We need to try to take the emotion out of it," Fred said. "I'm serious here. He's made an incredibly unselfish offer, and we should take the time to consider it properly."

"Is it unselfish?" Ginger queried.

"I know there's no such thing as a selfless act," Fred replied, "I've already thought of that. He feels terrible about what his father did, and he wants to make himself feel better."

Sandi frowned. "But surely it means by law he'd get half of the vineyard by being married to you?"

"He told me I could draw up any pre-nup I want, and that he wouldn't make a caveat that we have to keep him on—that would be up to us. He doesn't want the land. He wants to help us."

They all thought about that.

"He sounds too good to be true," Ginger said. "But actually, that wasn't what I meant when I asked if it was unselfish. I meant, do you really think he hasn't thought about what it would mean to be married to you, on a personal level?"

"What do you mean?"

Ginger's expression softened. "You'd be his wife. Don't you think that would change how you feel about him? And don't you think he knows that?"

Sandi's eyebrows rose. "You mean, he's hoping it might help Fred develop feelings for him?"

"Yeah. That's exactly what I meant."

Fred's heart banged, but she kept still, not wanting to give her feelings away. "I don't think so," she said calmly. "I know it's difficult for us to trust people at the moment. We've all been duped, and we're going to be suspicious of ulterior motives. And of course, I don't know him well, so I can't be certain there's nothing behind his offer. But he seems genuine. I truly believe he wants to help us and put right what his father did. He could have made all kinds of offers to me—he could have asked for half the money for himself, or said he'd marry me providing I agree to let him stay on as estate manager."

"But don't you see," Sandi insisted, "that's what makes it even more strange. It would have made more sense if he *had* stipulated that you keep him on. At least he would be getting something out of it. What's he getting out of this? Do we all really believe he's doing it out of the goodness of his heart?"

Fred's throat tightened. Sandi had not only lost her partner—she'd had to deal with his terrible betrayal and, hot on the heels of that, the knowledge that their mother had also betrayed them for many years. It was no wonder she was so afraid to trust.

But that didn't mean that Mac wasn't genuine. It was like rolling a dice—if you rolled a six the first time it didn't reduce the chance of rolling a six the next. And so it was with people—just because they'd all been terribly hurt by someone's cruel actions didn't mean that the next person who came along wouldn't have a heart of gold.

Equally, she warned herself, she had to go into this with open eyes. She had to be critical and careful, but it would be a mistake to turn her back on a genuine opportunity.

"When it comes down to it," she said, "what other choice do we have? I think we've all decided that we want to stay. I don't know about you two, but it's clear to me that Mac was right, and the place needs some serious money spent on it. Yes, we could get a couple of cheap cans of paint and give it the appearance that we've overhauled the place, but the locals would know, the people who work here would know. Mac would know. He might not stay, and we need him to stay. He knows the place inside out, and I don't think any of us can deny he knows his stuff where winemaking is concerned. He can make the vineyard a success again, I'm convinced of it, and if the vineyard's a success, the B&B and the restaurant will have the chance to be, too."

She tapped on the table. "But to do it properly, we need money. We could wait until we get residency, then apply for a loan, but do we really want to sink ourselves deep into debt? You heard what he said—forty to fifty thousand to really make some good changes. This would be a start, and providing we reinvest the majority of the profits we make, we'll be well on the way." She leaned forward to catch their gazes. "Do we really want to do this? To stay, to begin again, and try to make it work here? Or do we want to give up, sell, and go back to the U.K.?"

"I don't want to go back," Ginger said immediately.

"Neither do I," Sandi said, a bit more slowly. "But equally, I don't want you to give up your freedom for us, either. If this is the only way, I want you to be sure. Even if Mac's intentions are honorable, it doesn't change the fact that you'll be tied into the contract for two years. It's a long time, Fred. Are you sure that's what you want?"

Fred shrugged. "It is and it isn't. It'll take us that long, I suspect, to get this place the way we want it—the way it should be once again. I think two years will pass quickly. And look, even if it doesn't, and even if I were to meet a guy in the bay, if he was the sort of man who'd be interested in me, I'd expect him to understand why I made this decision. It wouldn't mean that I couldn't date anyone."

"I suppose." Sandi met her sister's gaze, and her lips curved up. "You really want to do this?"

"Fifty thousand dollars," Fred whispered. "Imagine what we could do with that!"

"Has Mac got two brothers?" Ginger grinned. "Imagine what we could do with a hundred and fifty thousand!"

They all giggled.

"Seriously, though," Ginger said, "what would we do with the fifty thousand? How would we decide where to spend it?"

"Well, I'd bring Mac in on that decision. If he's going to be our estate manager, we'll need his input, and he's the most informed person anyway. We need to work out what our profits are likely to be, and what else we need to invest in the vineyard to start the ball rolling, and then it should be clear what we can spare to put into the restaurant and the B&B. We all know the vineyard's important, but equally I want us all to have something to work with. There's no point in having a fantastic Cellar Door, but everything else looking like crap."

"I suppose." Ginger put her hand in the middle of the table, palm down. "So we're all agreed, then?"

Fred took a deep breath and put her hand on top of her sister's. "I'll take the rest of the day to think about it. But at the moment, yes, I think I should take Mac's offer."

They both looked at Sandi. With some reluctance, she reached out her hand and placed it on theirs. "As long as you're sure," she said. "Don't rush into it, Fred. If you feel you need a week or even longer to think about it, make sure you take the time."

"I will." Fred withdrew her hand. "Okay, I'm going up to the house to finish sorting out the bedrooms. I'll see you later."

"Yeah, see ya, Fred."

She walked out and headed up to the house. Her mind was buzzing, but she couldn't deny the feeling of excitement in her stomach at the knowledge that her sisters had agreed with the idea. They'd be able to stay!

She stopped at the gate to the house and looked across the vineyard, to where Blue Penguin Bay curved below them like a smile. Harry Cartwright had probably stood in this very spot at some point, looking at his vineyard, staring out at the Pacific Ocean. Had he thought of his family back in England very much? Had he wondered about his girls? He must have been devastated when he thought they'd chosen not to write back to him.

A lump formed in her throat, and she swallowed. He knew what Louise Cartwright was like—had he ever considered that she might be behind her daughters' lack of communication? Maybe he hadn't been able to bring himself to believe she could be that spiteful. Fred still had trouble believing it herself. In the way that Mac was convinced that his father's decision to destroy the original will had driven James MacDonald mad, she wondered whether her mother choosing to keep up the pretense that Harry had no interest in keeping in touch with his family had had some connection with her illness, and how bad she'd gotten over the years.

She thought about what Mac had said, about how Harry was still here somewhere, watching over her. And about the quote from *Gone with the Wind*, about land being the only thing in the world worth working for, worth fighting for, worth dying for. She liked that he felt the same way about Blue Penguin Bay that she did. The thought of him standing beside her, working with her to make the vineyard great once again, gave her a glow inside that she couldn't ignore.

But she would take the day to think about it, she promised herself. Or longer, if necessary. There was no need to make a decision on the spot, even if her sisters agreed it was a good idea.

*

For the rest of the day, she cleaned and tidied, getting rid of the last of the rubbish before making sure that all the wooden floors were scrubbed and the windows opened to let in the fresh air and cleanse away any of James's lingering presence.

She didn't see Mac, didn't see anyone, in fact, and thoroughly enjoyed herself, pleased at the end of the day to stand back and view her handiwork, and see the place looking spick and span.

Taking a can of Coke Zero out of the fridge, she went out and sat on the bench that faced the vineyard. It was around six, a few hours yet until sunset. The clouds had cleared from the morning, and although the breeze was cool, the sun was warm enough to sit without a jacket. The ripe grapes glowed like marbles, the green vines rich and lush. She could almost taste the wine they'd make.

Her *turangawaewae*. Yes, she could easily make this her place to stand.

Someone exited the barrel hall, and she saw him walking toward the house. Her heart rate immediately sped up, but she stayed seated, letting him see that she was watching him walk. He had a casual roll, his hands in the pockets of his jeans. His hair looked as if it hadn't been brushed for a fortnight. His arms shone in the late rays of the sun, gleaming an impressive bronze. He looked like a god.

"Hey," he said as he came through the gate. He walked across and sat beside her.

"Hey." She smiled. "How's your day been?"

"Productive. Getting ready for the harvest. We're about there. We'll start on Monday, I think. How about you?" His ocean-blue eyes surveyed her.

She stifled a shiver. "Finished the bedrooms. The house is looking good."

He looked pleased. "Ah, well done. I'm sorry I left you to it. I meant to help with that."

"It's okay. It gave me time to think. I talked to Sandi and Ginger this morning, by the way. And I've been thinking all day."

"Oh?" His gaze met hers. And even though she knew this was strictly business, and even though she knew it shouldn't mean anything, deep down she felt a flutter of pleasure at the hope in his eyes.

"Mmm," she said. "And the answer's yes."

Chapter Fourteen

"Mac!" The tall, gray-haired woman who'd opened the door flung out her arms to encourage a hug.

Mac did so, kissing her cheek at the same time. Jackie Coulthard was a qualified celebrant. She was also a friend of his mother's, and he'd known her for over twenty years.

"Jackie, this is Fred," he told her, stepping back to let Fred come forward.

Jackie shook her hand and said, "Welcome, Fred," but he could see her assessing Fred shrewdly. His mother had told him that Jackie was uneasy about performing the ceremony, and that she wanted to talk to them both before they went ahead. He wasn't sure if it was Jackie who was uncertain or his mother, but he was prepared to give them the benefit of the doubt and answer a few questions.

He was aware, though, that inside he felt like a sixteen-year-old introducing his girlfriend to his old aunt. He wanted Jackie to like Fred. That, in itself, interested him.

"Come in, come in." She beckoned them into the house, which was large and impressive. The living room had huge north-facing windows that overlooked Russell and, beyond, the curve of Blue Penguin Bay. He could just see the terracotta buildings of the estate high on the hill opposite.

She led them to a cream sofa and sat opposite them in an armchair. In front of them, three cups and a pot of tea rested on a tray, along with a plate of homemade cookies. Outside, it was raining, and the drops peppered the windows and bounced off the deck.

He sat back, conscious of Fred beside him sitting on the edge, her spine stiff. He still couldn't believe she'd agreed to go ahead with his crazy plan.

Jackie poured them all tea as they chatted about the weather and what Fred thought of the bay. When they all had a cup in their hands and were munching on cookies, Jackie finally broached the subject.

"So… you two are thinking of getting married."

He swallowed the mouthful and cleared his throat. "Yes. And we'd like you to do it."

"Okay. Well, Megan's given me some insight into why you're making this decision, but I'd like to hear your side of it."

So Mac gave her a rundown, explaining about the fake will, how James had spent all the money, and how he himself had contacted Fred when he'd discovered Harry's letter.

Jackie listened to it all, sipping her tea, her gaze flicking occasionally to Fred, who confirmed each detail with a nod of her head.

"All right," Jackie said when he'd finished. "So, Fred, you need to show a marriage certificate to your lawyer to access your funds."

"Yes."

"But beyond that, there was nothing else stipulated about the relationship."

"No."

Jackie nodded and pressed her lips together, her gaze meeting Mac's.

"Come on," he said softly, "be honest. I don't want you to do anything you're uncomfortable with. Is part of your role to assess the intention behind a couple's decision to marry?"

Jackie put down her cup. "No. I've thought about it a lot, and I've read the code of ethics and professional standards. It says that we should preserve the clients' rights to personal choice and decision-making. We're supposed to provide guidance about the ceremony, and take into account the couple's beliefs and traditions. I am conscious that if this were a religious ceremony, the priest or whoever was marrying you would have a duty to assess the couple's readiness for marriage, and whether they understood the solemnity of the vows. However, I don't believe it's my job to decide the depth of feeling in a relationship. There are places all over the world where arranged marriages are common, and I've actually officiated in two of those with couples from Vanuatu, so in that sense I don't see why this is any different."

She surveyed him with a frown. "Except that it's you, Mac. I'm a little disappointed in you. That you think so little of marriage."

He shifted on the sofa under Jackie's cool gaze, continuing to feel sixteen. "I don't think little of it at all. One day I hope I'll get married properly, and I'll write my own vows and do all the 'in sickness and in health' stuff, and I'll mean every word." He forced himself not to glance at Fred, who was looking up at him. "But that's not what this is about. I have to do something, Jackie. What my father did—it hurts me, physically. I have to try to put it right. The land belongs to Fred and her sisters, and I'm convinced that if Harry had known what my father was going to do, he wouldn't have tied up the girls' money in this way. I need to do something."

"All right," Jackie said gently. "I understand. I guess I am a little puzzled as to why you didn't choose a celebrant you didn't know. You wouldn't have to explain yourself then. Why not just pretend, wouldn't that have been easier?"

Fred spoke up then. "We thought about it. Both of us feel awkward asking a celebrant to marry us knowing it's for show, and especially with you being a friend of Mac's mother—I hope you don't see it as an insult. But I think it would be worse to be married by a stranger who would assume that we're in a relationship and genuinely want to commit to each other for the rest of our lives. We do both value marriage as an institution. We don't want our vows to include statements about 'till death us do part' that we have no intention of obeying. It doesn't feel right."

Her cheeks flushed. Mac had to fight not to reach out and feel the warmth of her skin. He envied the man to whom she would eventually pledge her life and vow to love and cherish forever. Inside, he felt an odd twinge at the thought that they wouldn't be exchanging the traditional vows. He'd never given marriage a lot of thought in the past. How would it feel to be promising Fred that he'd stay by her side forever? That he'd never love another woman except her?

Conscious that the room had gone quiet, he glanced at Jackie. She sipped her tea, and he had the feeling she was hiding a smile behind her cup. "Okay," she said. "You understand the legal obligations of what you're getting into? That although yours might be a business relationship, it doesn't change the legal, binding aspect of it?"

They both nodded.

"All right. We'll keep the vows simple. I won't ask you anything that you have to lie to answer—we'll stick to just what you need to get it done legally, which is surprisingly little."

"Sounds great," Mac said, feeling a swell of relief, and Fred's slow exhalation told him she felt the same.

He'd be able to put things right at last. "Thank you," he mouthed to Jackie.

She said nothing, just smiled and nodded, and then began to talk about the weather again.

*

"You're absolutely sure about this?" Sam asked.

It was just over a week later, Saturday eighteenth of March, twelve thirty p.m., and Mac was standing on the deck outside the restaurant, waiting for his bride. Scully sat by his side with a bow in her collar, the prettiest bridesmaid he'd ever seen.

"I'm sure." Mac smiled at the strangeness of that reply. Since he'd first made the suggestion to Fred, he'd not had a single moment of doubt. It felt like the right thing to do, and he hadn't regretted it for a second.

"Weirdo." Sam stuffed his hands in the pockets of his trousers. "I can't believe you actually volunteered to get hitched."

Mac grinned. After dating an ex whose sole goal had appeared to be to get his ring on her finger, Sam had developed an allergy to anything wedding related.

"Thanks," Mac said. "For being my best man, such as it is." Sam was there to be a witness.

"Yeah, well, it's not quite the role I'd anticipated. I thought I was going to be able to do the whole kit and kaboodle, you know, make jokes about your first dates, embarrass you, embarrass the bride… Doesn't have quite the same effect when the two of you don't give a damn about each other."

Mac gave his best mate a wry look. There was an undernote of warning in Sam's words. He didn't agree with what his friend was doing, although he would never say in so many words.

"I do give a damn about her," Mac said. "I wouldn't be doing this if I didn't."

"I guess. Not sure you can say the same about her. It makes her a bit of a cold fish, if you ask me."

"Careful," Mac said. "That's my bride-to-be you're talking about."

"Mac…"

"Sam, relax. We're here to sign a business contract, that's all. It doesn't mean anything. Yeah, it's a shame it's binding for two years, but it won't change a single thing about our daily lives. Nobody will even notice."

He'd taken every care to make sure that was the case, not wanting Fred to have any worries about what they were about to do. He'd taken Fred to meet Jace Hart, his lawyer in Kerikeri, who also happened to have been Harry's lawyer, and who was aware of the problems with the fake will. Jace, and Fred's lawyer in the U.K., had confirmed all that was required was a legal marriage certificate for Fred to access the funds tied up in her inheritance, and there was no clause that demanded to know when she'd met her husband, or how long they intended to stay together. Jace had also drawn up a pre-nup for Fred on Mac's insistence, in which he signed away any claim on her money or her share of the estate. She'd then made Jace draw up one for Mac in which she'd done the same, making it clear that the two of them were to lead individual lives and have no claim on the other's money or property.

"I'm still kinda surprised she didn't want all the paraphernalia of a real wedding," Sam said. "I thought women liked dressing up."

"Fred's not like that. We agreed that, as it was a business deal, there was no point in arranging anything special."

Sam turned his astute gaze on his friend. "So why is it happening here and not in the registry office in Kaikohe?"

For a second, Mac found himself tongue-tied. He could see in Sam's eyes his suspicion that Mac had feelings for the woman with whom he was about to tie the knot.

He was right, of course. But it was irrelevant. Just because he liked Fred, it didn't mean this wasn't about business.

"It might not be a love match," he explained, "but it still has meaning. It feels right for it to happen at the vineyard, and Fred feels the same. I want it to be a celebration of the end of hostility between our families."

"Very Henry Tudor," Sam stated.

Mac laughed. "Yeah, I guess."

"As long as you're sure," Sam said softly.

"I'm sure." Mac looked out across the vineyard. "I had to do something. If they'd turned up and been three spoilt brats who'd yelled at me for stealing their fortune, I might not have felt so inclined to help. But I think you'll understand when you meet them."

"I hope so. I'm guessing there must be something special about them if they're Harry's girls." Sam had been fond of Harry

Cartwright—they both had. "I wonder what he'd think of this 'transaction'," Sam said, putting air quotes around the word.

"I hope he'd be touched that I'm trying to put things right," Mac replied. Poor Harry. Betrayed by both the man he'd thought was his best friend, and his own wife. Abandoned by all those he'd thought loved him. Mac's throat tightened. If nothing else, he wanted to help Harry's daughter get what she deserved.

"Mac?"

He turned to see Jackie waiting at the edge of the deck. She was wearing a dark-gray suit and a white blouse with a pink carnation pinned to the lapel of her jacket.

"Jackie." He smiled and walked forward to kiss her cheek. "Thanks for doing this."

She stepped back and held his hands, giving him a shrewd look. "You certain you know what you're doing?"

"Don't start," he scolded.

She squeezed his hands and released them. "All right. As long as you're sure."

"My son doesn't do anything until he's thought it through," said a woman who'd just rounded the corner behind her. "At least, that's what I keep telling myself."

"Hey, Mum." He bent and kissed his mother on the cheek. "You look lovely."

Megan MacDonald wore a pretty turquoise dress, and she had a matching clip in her hair with a spray of butterflies that danced in the breeze. "Thank you."

"You didn't have to dress up," he said.

"Hey, this is probably the only time I'll be a mother-of-the-groom," she said playfully. "I'm going to make the most of it."

Mac smiled, for the first time feeling a twinge of uneasiness. It was odd, but even though they all knew this was about business, everyone had made an effort with their appearance, even Sam, who'd shunned his usual jeans and All Blacks top for a pair of smart black trousers and a checked shirt, although he hadn't gone as far as donning a tie.

Mac himself had also chosen black trousers and a white shirt, and he'd shaved and was wearing his best watch and smart shoes. Now, he wondered why he'd made that decision. It must be the word 'wedding', he thought. Even though everyone knew what was going on, and even though nowadays fewer people were getting married and everyone kept saying the institution had little meaning, there was something about the exchanging of vows that you just had to take seriously.

He scratched his chin. Maybe this hadn't been such a good idea.

It was too late to think about it now, though, because the door from the garden to the restaurant had opened, and Fred and her sisters were coming through.

His lips curved up as they crossed the restaurant and came onto the deck. All three of them had attempted to look casual, but they'd obviously taken time over their appearance.

Sandi wore a sleeveless blue dress, her hair falling over her shoulder in a single braid. Ginger wore cream wide-leg trousers and a navy blouse with large cream spots, and although her blonde hair hung loose, she'd pulled back a few strands with a clip bearing a small navy flower.

Fred was wearing a floor-length Indian-style skirt that changed from light orange on her hips to a deep russet red where it brushed the deck. Numerous sequins and beads sewn into the pleated material shimmered in the sunlight. She'd topped it with a short white tunic, and she wore flat red sandals. Her hair hung to her waist, but she'd plaited two thin braids at her temples and joined them at the back with a clip, making her look almost medieval, and bringing to mind Sam's jest about Henry VII.

The past week, they'd started harvesting the Pinot Gris and Chardonnay grapes, and the two of them had worked flat out alongside the seasonal employees, Fred beside him more often than not, listening to everything he said as he supervised the grape picking and showed her the process from vine to bottle. It was with no small sense of irony that he'd thought how well they worked together considering what they were about to do.

She hadn't mentioned the kiss again, though, and neither had he.

"Hey," he said as she walked up to him. He'd wondered whether she would look nervous, concerned that they were about to make a mistake, but to his surprise she gave him a big smile, her eyes dancing.

"Hello, husband-to-be," she teased.

He laughed and held out his hand, enjoying the feel of her fingers when she slipped them into his. "Mum, I'd like you to meet my bride." He drew Fred over to Megan.

"Hello, Mrs. MacDonald." Fred cast him a scolding glance. Her cheeks flushed a little. She was embarrassed to face his mother. Aw, he thought. That was sweet.

"Hello, Fred, and please, call me Megan." His mother kissed her on the cheek. "I'm very pleased to meet you, even if these are rather strange circumstances."

"Just a bit." Flustered, Fred turned to the two young women waiting behind her. "These are my sisters, Ginger and Sandi."

Mac introduced them to Jackie, and also to Sam, who stood to one side, watching them all quietly. Mac was expecting a few wisecracks, some teasing from the guy who was so certain the three girls were secretly planning to destroy his best mate. He half expected him to query Fred on her prospects. But Sam stayed silent and polite, and for that, anyway, Mac was thankful.

"Okay," Jackie said, leading them forward to where Mac had placed four chairs facing the vineyard, and a small table to one side. Neither of them had seen any point in organizing flowers or music, but he had designed a display for the table out of flowers from the garden and a few small bunches of grapes from the vineyard. He wasn't sure why he'd done that.

"Shall we start?"

Mac met Fred's eyes. They looked a little feverish, and her cheeks were still flushed, but she nodded and smiled, so he said, "Sure."

His mother sat next to Sam, and Ginger and Sandi sat the other side. Jackie stood in front of them, and gestured for Mac and Fred to stand before her. Scully sat with Sam, loving having all her friends around.

"So." She glanced around at them all, and smiled. "My name is Jacqueline Coulthard, and am the celebrant at today's wedding. Mac has requested a brief ceremony, bearing in mind that this is a business transaction, so I won't be going through my usual romantic spiel. However, I will start the way I usually do, in telling you that I am authorized by law to solemnize marriages according to law. I am supposed to remind you of the solemn and binding nature of the relationship you are about to enter. Marriage, according to New Zealand law, is the union of two people, to the exclusion of all others, voluntarily entered into for life. The nature of your business relationship does not change the legal aspect of this relationship. Do you both understand?"

Fred cleared her throat and nodded. "Yes."

"Yes," Mac said. He met her gaze. She wasn't smiling now, but she didn't look away.

"Okay," Jackie continued. "You've decided not to have any readings, songs, poems, or anything like that, and you won't be exchanging rings, so there are only the vows to say. Are you both ready? This is going to be quick—now is the time to speak up if you need more time."

Fred shook her head. "I'm ready."

Mac glanced at Sam, who raised an eyebrow, then at his mother, who smiled. He nodded at Jackie.

"Mac, you first please," Jackie said. "Will you repeat after me? I call upon the persons here present to witness that I, Eamon James MacDonald, take you, Winifred Rose Cartwright, to be my lawful wedded wife."

Mac took a deep breath, looked into Fred's eyes, and repeated the words.

Then it was Fred's turn.

"I call upon the persons here present," she began, her voice barely audible. She cleared her throat and continued. "To witness that I, Winifred Rose Cartwright, take you, Eamon James MacDonald, to be my lawful wedded husband."

Silence fell. Mac looked into Fred's eyes. They were like forest pools, deep and green with brown shadows, and for a moment time fell away and he could almost feel her in his arms again, her mouth soft beneath his, her hands splaying on his chest.

Was Harry there, watching them? Did he know how Mac felt about her, deep in his heart?

"I now pronounce you man and wife," Jackie said. And then, a touch of mischief in her voice, she added, "Mac, you may kiss the bride."

Chapter Fifteen

To Fred's relief, everyone laughed at Jackie's comment. Mac sent the celebrant a wry look, then turned his smiling gaze to Fred, lifted her hand in his, and kissed the tips of her fingers.

Fred felt her face flush, although it was an innocent gesture, and his lips barely touched her. She was married. She was married! It made her head spin.

Jackie led them to the small table where she laid out the contract, and they spent a few moments dotting the 'i's and crossing the 't's, with Sam and Sandi as witnesses. Fred signed her name in a daze. Over the past week, she'd spent most of her free time telling herself that this was purely business, and it didn't mean anything. They weren't promising to stay together forever, or to love no other for the rest of their days.

As everyone stood, however, and started making their way inside the restaurant where they'd planned to have dinner to celebrate the arrangement, Fred's heart raced as she watched the tall, dark-haired man she'd just pledged herself to talking to his best mate. She watched Mac dip his head slightly to listen to what Sam was saying. She surveyed his relaxed pose, the way his shirt stretched across his broad shoulders, how his eyes crinkled at the edges when he smiled, and she felt a little dizzy. She'd married him. Holy moly.

It meant nothing.

Why didn't it feel like nothing?

Sam glanced at her, caught her gaze, and smiled. Mac turned to look at her, and he walked over and studied her face.

"You okay?" he asked.

"Yeah." She sounded breathless, even to herself.

"All right." He held out his hand. "Come on."

She took it, letting him lead her inside, trying not to panic. Jackie was saying goodbye to the others, as she had another wedding in the bay shortly.

"Thank you," Fred said to her when she came over. "I know it was against the rules, so to speak, and I appreciate your understanding."

"Best of luck," Jackie replied. "I hope it works out, for both of you."

Fred opened her mouth to ask what she meant, but Jackie was already turning away to say goodbye to Mac. What did she hope would work out? The business arrangement? Or the marriage itself?

Shaking her head, Fred walked over to where her sisters were talking to Megan MacDonald and Sam. It was the first time she'd met either of them, and she felt shy talking to both Mac's mother and his best friend, the two people in his life who would probably be most wary of what he'd done.

But Megan was laughing and her expression when she smiled at Fred certainly didn't seem hostile.

"I was just saying to your sisters," Megan explained, "how I hope this goes some way to putting right what James did." Her smile faded a little, and Fred was reminded that the two of them had divorced when Mac was young, so clearly Megan had gained an understanding of James's worth many years ago.

"It does," Fred said amiably. "Mac is very generous, and I will always be grateful to him for what he's done."

"So, what are you going to do with the money?" Megan led the way to the table that had been laid for them. Amber, the young woman from the village who had worked in the B&B and whom Mac had kept on, had placed the centerpiece that Mac had made in the middle of the round table, and she was waiting now, smiling, as they took their seats.

"We've all been talking a lot about it," Fred said. Mac took a seat opposite her, while Sam sat next to her. "We agree that new equipment for the vineyard is our priority, so some of it will go on that. But we also want to allocate a good portion toward the B&B and the restaurant. It's important that we all have some cash to work with, and that the whole place gets at least a fresh coat of paint."

"And you're keeping Mac on as estate manager?" Megan leaned back so Amber could pour a glass of Chardonnay for her.

"Yes, of course."

"Because you feel beholden to him?" Megan asked.

"No." Fred kept her gaze even. "Because he's an excellent viticulturist and clearly knows his stuff. I'm interested in the business and would like to be able to make decisions about our wine, but I need someone at the heart of things who knows what he's doing, and who can teach me properly."

She stopped, conscious of Mac watching her. Something in his blue eyes was giving her goosebumps, especially when she said, *who can teach me properly.* "About wine," she added without thinking. Was it her imagination, or did his lips twitch? She was sure she saw him glance at Sam, and Sam's eyebrows rise.

No, no, she was imagining it. Accepting a glass from Amber, she took a large gulp, desperate to calm her nerves. *It's just a piece of paper, Fred. There's no small print, no magical clause that's going to whisk away your freedom. Get a grip.*

For a while, she sat back and listened to the others talk, and gradually she relaxed and began to enjoy herself. Their worries really were over, for a while at least. Her sisters were happy and laughing. Megan was obviously pleased that the curse her husband had laid on the estate appeared to have lifted. Sam was teasing her sisters, especially Ginger, who was giving as good as she got and thoroughly enjoying herself. And Mac… The cloud that had been hanging over him since she'd arrived appeared to have lifted, and he actually seemed happy.

It was because he was staying at the vineyard, she thought. How lovely that she'd found someone who adored the place as much as she did. And he'd been in the bay for years, since he was born in fact. He had ties to the place too, and she knew he'd open a vein and pour his lifeblood into the soil if he thought it would help to grow better grapes.

He was listening to Sam talking to Ginger.

"What do you do for a living?" Ginger asked.

"I'm a baker." Sam popped a green-lipped mussel in his mouth and licked his fingers.

Ginger's eyebrows rose. "Please tell me you live next to a butcher and a candlestick maker."

That made Sam laugh, and Mac smiled. Then he happened to glance over at Fred and caught her looking at him. Embarrassed, she went to look away, but found she couldn't, caught like a butterfly in a net.

Their vows had contained only the statements required by law, and there had been none of the elaborate phrases she knew most brides and grooms said to each other. For better, for worse, for richer, for poorer, in sickness and in health. To love and to cherish. Until death do us part. And yet even the one sentence she'd had to repeat had contained a ring of finality. *I, Winifred Rose Cartwright, take you, Eamon James MacDonald, to be my lawful wedded husband.*

Jackie had said, *Marriage is the union of two people, to the exclusion of all others, voluntarily entered into for life.*

Legally, she'd promised to honor that statement. It was only now, as she looked into his eyes, that she fully felt in her heart what she'd done.

Oh shit.

Mac's smile held a touch of sympathy, as if he understood what was going through her mind. To her surprise, he winked at her before turning his gaze back to the others.

She inhaled deeply and blew out the breath. Everything was going to be okay. She just needed time to come to terms with it.

An hour passed, while Amber brought out plate after plate of food, and their glasses were repeatedly filled.

Fred ate until she was full, but she was careful not to drink as much as she had during the night they'd had the wine tasting. She was going to have to be careful, living on a vineyard! It would be almost as bad as working in a chocolate shop.

Pushing away the dish on which she'd had her dessert—an ice cream that had been pleasant enough, although she knew Ginger would be making some twice as nice—she saw that Sam had risen to take a walk outside. Leaving Mac telling a story to his mother and her sisters, she rose and went out, leaving the deck, and crossing the grass to where he was standing, looking down at the bay.

"Hey," she said as he turned and saw her coming. "You mind me joining you?"

"Of course not." He smiled. "That was a nice meal."

"It was okay. Ginger's food will knock your socks off."

He grinned. "Yeah, I bet."

They continued walking alongside the vineyard, down to where the ground fell away to the sea. She felt a little shy, knowing that he knew Mac so well. He was a good-looking guy, very boy-next-door, with ruffled hair and brown eyes. He also smelled of warm bread—

presumably he'd been in the bakery that morning. Well, there were a lot worse things a man could smell of.

"Thanks for coming," Fred said. "I just wanted to say... I know you're Mac's best mate, and I'm sure you must have had some concerns about what we've done. I hope I've allayed any fears you've had."

He gave her an appraising look. "Not really, no."

That gave her pause for thought. "Oh. Um..."

He sighed. "Okay, I admit that before I met you all, I couldn't understand why he'd made the offer. Now, I can see it. You're all genuine, lovely girls, and I can see how you won him over. And there's no doubt he feels better. He was in a dark place after he discovered what his father had done, and for the first time he looks as if he thinks the world might be somewhere he wants to live."

"But..."

"But that wasn't why I was worried."

"Why are you worried?"

Sam stopped and shoved his hands in his pockets. "Because he has feelings for you."

Her eyebrows rose slowly. "I'm sure you're wrong."

"No, I'm right."

"He said that?"

"No. But I've known him long enough to be surprised at the dazed look in his eyes. He hasn't had that in a long time. Maybe ever."

Fred's jaw had dropped. "Sam..."

"He's telling himself that this marriage means nothing, and that it's going to make no difference to the way you feel about him, but I don't know if his heart believes it. I'm worried that deep down, he's hoping that because you married him, it might make you more inclined to..." His voice trailed off.

"To..." she said, her voice a squeak.

He shrugged.

To what? To fall in love with him? To stay with him? Her heart banged hard on her ribs, and for a moment she felt dizzy.

"Don't break his heart," Sam said. "Don't lead him on and let him think he has a chance."

The blood that had previously drained from her face rushed back, making her cheeks burn.

"Unless he has," Sam added, studying her blush with interest.

"Yes. I mean no. I mean… this is none of your business, Sam, and I object to you sticking your nose in where it doesn't belong!" she snapped.

He gave a short laugh. "Right. That's put me in my place." He looked more amused than angry, though.

Fred pressed a hand to her forehead. "Oh God. I shouldn't have said that. I swear, Sam, I have no intention—"

"Hey, don't worry about it." He put a comforting hand on her shoulder. "I shouldn't have said anything. I'm sorry. You're absolutely right, it's none of my business."

He turned back to face the restaurant. "Come on. I should get going anyway. Let's head back." He started talking about the harvest, and Fred did her best to answer his questions as they crossed back to the building. Inside, though, her head was whirling. *He has feelings for you.* Was Sam right? Surely not. She hadn't known Mac long enough for him to develop feelings for her. She didn't believe in love at first sight, and had always thought that people who protested they did were fooling themselves.

And yet… She couldn't deny the tingle she'd felt when she'd looked into his eyes that very first day on arriving at the vineyard.

They entered the restaurant, and she shoved all thought of Sam's comments away as they started saying their goodbyes to him and Megan. Sam had nothing to worry about. Mac didn't have feelings for her. It was possible he found her attractive, and she'd be happy to admit the same, because what was there about him to dislike? Both Sandi and Ginger had said he was gorgeous—and Fred wouldn't deny she thought the same. It was also true that he seemed to like them all, and he'd said that was the reason why he'd made the suggestion to get married, so he could help them.

But did he have feelings for her? Feelings that went beyond initial attraction and pity for her plight?

Of course not. The idea was preposterous.

Chapter Sixteen

Mac had seen Fred leave the restaurant to walk with Sam. When they returned, he saw her blush, noticed Sam's amused gaze, and raised an eyebrow at him, but Sam just shrugged and said he had to go.

"Break a leg," Sam said, shaking his hand.

"Goodbye," Mac replied firmly, hoping Fred hadn't overheard. Luckily, she was saying farewell to his mother.

"Stay in touch," was all Sam said to Fred as he bent to kiss her cheek. He said goodbye to Sandi, teased Ginger when she knocked over the table decoration as she came around to say goodbye, and headed out to the taxi waiting in the car park.

Mac glanced at Fred, but she was looking down, and he frowned suspiciously. "You okay?" he murmured. When she just nodded, he said, "Did Sam say something to upset you?"

She looked up at him then, and gave a quick shake of her head. "No, no. It wasn't him. I made a fool of myself and got embarrassed." She gave a little laugh.

"With Sam?" Mac was puzzled. Sam may have had his suspicions about Fred's motives, but he was a nice guy, and he'd have cut off his right arm rather than make someone feel uncomfortable.

She waved a hand though, clearly not wanting to elaborate.

"I'm off then," his mother said, coming up to them.

"Okay, Mum, thanks for coming." He kissed her.

"Best of luck to you both," she said. "I'm sure you're all going to make the place into a huge success."

"We'll do our best," Fred said.

Mac walked his mother out to the taxi. "I'll be down later. Going to check out the vineyard first."

"Of course you are." Megan glanced over her shoulder at where the three sisters were standing talking inside the restaurant. "She's lovely, Mac."

"She is." Mac smiled, his gaze caressing Fred's slender form in her white tunic and long skirt. She was laughing at something Ginger had said, the dimples appearing in her cheeks.

"You want to keep her?"

Mac's eyes widened, and he looked back at his mother. "What?"

Megan smiled. "Give her time. Let her come to her own conclusions. If it's meant to be, it'll happen when the time's right."

"Mum, I don't know what you think—"

She rested a finger on his lips. "I'll see you later." Then she turned and got into the other waiting taxi, and it pulled away, leaving Mac standing there with his jaw sagging.

He shut it with a snap. His mother was wrong. He liked Fred, and he was thrilled to think he'd been able to help her. But he hadn't married her with the intention of making it permanent.

He returned his gaze to the girls. Ginger had left—he suspected she'd gone into the kitchen, because if she disappeared that was normally where she could be found.

Fred and Sandi had wandered to the doorway overlooking the vineyard. Mac walked back into the restaurant and picked up his wine glass, which still held an inch of brick-red Merlot. He sipped it, watching the girls, swirling the wine around his mouth, enjoying the flavor.

He was married. He had the contract in his back pocket, their signatures declaring they'd taken a pledge to one another. The union of two people, to the exclusion of all others.

Heat rushed through him, and he felt a tad dizzy. What had he done? He'd meant this to be like the sale of a car, a scribble on a bit of paper to cheat the stupid clause that Harry had, for some reason, made in his will. But all of a sudden, it felt so much more than that.

Mac hadn't given any thought to why Harry had made that clause, but for the first time he wondered what Fred's father would think of the fact that Mac had, on purpose, treated his real will with disrespect.

He'd meant this marriage to put things right, but he couldn't shake the feeling that Harry was glaring down at him from his cloud, furious that yet again his wishes had been flouted.

Had Mac followed in his father's footsteps? Maybe what he'd done was as bad as what James had done.

He felt a swell of nausea, and had to take a deep breath to subdue it. No, he wasn't like his father. He refused to believe it. James had faked the will with every intention of cheating the girls out of their inheritance. Mac had married Fred to put things right. That was the difference.

Harry had made that clause in the hope of encouraging his daughters to find their Mr. Right and settle down, but he had been a decent guy, and he would have understood why Mac had done what he'd done, with good intentions.

Still, he couldn't shake his uneasiness at the thought that he was making a mockery of the institution of marriage. He frowned, giving a cynical laugh as he knocked back the last of the wine. Since when had he become Mr. Principled? His parents had divorced when he was two. His friends were unmarried and didn't seem bothered about it. It was the twenty-first century, in New Zealand—marriage was outdated. It didn't mean anything anymore.

Deep down, though, he didn't believe that. He wasn't religious, and had no problem with the notion of a couple divorcing if they felt that a marriage hadn't worked out—what was the point in staying together and making both of you miserable? Life was far too short for that. But he still felt that putting a ring on a girl's finger was a step he would like to take one day. It demonstrated commitment. It was a symbol of the promise that, at that moment, you were determined you were going to love her forever. Forsaking all others.

Fred wore no ring. There had been no lavish exchange of vows, no promise to love and honor, and certainly no promise to obey. His lips curved up briefly at the thought. But the commitment was there, all the same. Could he honestly look at the certificate in his pocket and decide it was any less meaningful than a promise he would make to the girl of his dreams? It certainly wasn't any less legal. If he walked out now, went into the bay, and slept with the first woman he met, he'd be breaking that promise.

It was just a bit of paper.

The trouble was, it didn't feel like just a bit of paper. There was no ring on his finger, but he could imagine what it would feel like to have one, a constant reminder of the girl who'd declared you were her Mr. Right. To love and to cherish. Until death do us part.

Fred turned and he saw her inhale, then smile. He walked across the restaurant and out onto the deck.

"Hey," she said. "Hubby."

That made him laugh. "Hey, ole ball and chain."

"Yeah, that's not going to get old anytime soon," she said wryly. "Oh well, it's all done."

"No regrets?" Sandi said.

"Nope." They'd made the step—there was no point in admitting how he was feeling.

"Are you going down to the vines?" Fred asked him.

"Yeah. Thought I'd do one last check." The seasonal pickers—mostly students, and often from abroad—worked on Saturdays until four, and it had just gone three p.m.

"I'll come with you. See you later," she said to her sister.

"All right." Sandi turned to go, then stopped. "Hey, guys?"

They both paused and glanced at her.

"Thanks," she said. "Ginger and I... we both appreciate what you've done. It can't have been an easy decision."

Mac shrugged. "It wasn't that tough."

Out of the corner of his eye, he saw Fred's lips curve up, but she didn't say anything.

"See you later," Sandi said, and went back into the restaurant.

Fred watched her go, flicked him a glance, and then they turned and started walking down toward the vines, Scully at their side.

They walked for a little way in silence. It was a beautiful early autumn day, warm and fine. Fred reached out and plucked a couple of grapes from a hanging bunch as they passed, giving one to him, and he bit into it, enjoying the flood of sweetness in his mouth.

"Are you okay?" she asked, surprising him.

"Yeah." He smiled at her. "Why wouldn't I be?"

"You've been a little quiet. I wondered whether you were regretting it?"

"No." He wiped his mouth with the back of his hand, and shoved his hands in his pockets. "Nothing like that." He decided it was best to be honest, though. "It did cross my mind that your dad might be angry with me."

"I doubt it. He would know you're trying to put things right."

"I hope so."

"It's odd though, isn't it," she said. "What we've done... It wasn't until I said the words that it hit me what we were doing."

"I know what you mean." He glanced at her, watching her long hair swing forward when she bent to hook a vine back on the string. "Fred, I hope you don't think that I believe marriage isn't a serious commitment. Proper marriage, I mean."

She stopped and turned her bright hazel eyes on him. "Mac, it's none of my business what you think of marriage."

He ran a hand through his hair, his stomach in a knot. "I guess, theoretically. But it's important to me that you understand."

"Why?"

That threw him. "I don't know."

They exchanged a long, long glance. Then they both turned and continued walking.

Fred didn't say anything more until they reached the group picking the grapes, and neither did he.

*

When they'd finished making sure all the grapes had been transported up to the sheds, they headed back up, pausing when they got to where the path forked.

"I think maybe it's time I moved out," Mac said awkwardly. "I don't like that I'm still in the house. It belongs to you girls."

"Mac, it makes perfect sense that you're here while the harvest is on. We're just fine in the B&B, we're quite comfortable, and it's not ready to open to visitors yet. We need a while to get it up to scratch, plus I want to spend some time redecorating the house before Ginger and I move in. Sandi's going to take the B&B flat, so it'll just be the two of us. But there's no rush."

"I suppose. But we're going to need to make a statement with Jace on Monday that we live at separate addresses so we can start the two-year process rolling. I'll be saying I've moved back to Mum's, and I'll give her address for now."

"Oh, yeah, of course." She looked slightly bewildered. "Wow, that must be the quickest marriage in history."

He laughed and scuffed the ground with his heel. "I'll make an appointment with Jace, shall I? He'll be able to finalize the condition of the will and release the money to you."

"Yes. That would be good."

Suddenly, they were as polite as strangers. Which was what they were, he thought, somewhat sadly. The piece of paper in his pocket hadn't changed that.

"What are you up to tomorrow?" he asked.

"We're going out exploring." The three of them had bought a car a few days before, a station wagon with plenty of space in the back for bringing back purchases from the town, comfortable enough if they traveled any distance. "We haven't seen much of the Northland yet, and we were saying how it's going to be important for us to make sure we take time off when we're working where we live, so we're going to go out every Sunday somewhere different. Tomorrow it's up to Doubtless Bay."

"That's a great idea."

"Yeah. Well, I'm sure I'll see you about, but if not, I'll be out in the sheds at eight on Monday. I guess I'll see you then."

"Okay."

She hesitated, and for a brief second, he thought she was going to lift up and kiss his cheek. Then she gave a brief smile, turned, and walked away.

He watched her until she disappeared into the B&B, then he walked up the path to the bench out the front of the house that faced the vineyard. He sat and leaned forward, elbows on his knees, hands loosely clasped, letting Scully lick his fingers.

He felt angry, and he didn't know why. Was it at Fred? He didn't think so. Maybe it was more at the situation.

What had he expected? He truly hadn't agreed to marry her with the thought that it would turn into a real relationship.

Or had he? Maybe deep down, he'd thought she'd be so grateful to him that she'd... what? Fall into his arms? Declare he was the one she'd been waiting for?

Dropping his head, he sank his hands into his hair. He'd known her exactly ten days. There was something seriously wrong with him for him to turn to the first woman who'd smiled at him, get down on one knee, and propose to her.

It wasn't like that, of course it wasn't like that. But even so, he felt immensely stupid. He couldn't lie to himself. He felt disappointed. It was idiotic and it made no sense at all, but he was disappointed that the day had ended like this. It was just a bit of paper, but it had changed him, changed the way he felt about her. Or maybe it had just clarified it, named it, brought it into being. It had switched on a light inside him, illuminating the emotions swirling in his heart.

Around him, the light slowly faded, the moon rose, the air became cool. But Mac stayed sitting there for a long, long time.

Chapter Seventeen

The days flew by.

Ginger took over the running of the restaurant and discovered that the difficult Phil was much happier as her sous chef, and in the end the two of them worked side by side to redevelop the menu and revamp the kitchen.

Sandi spent her days painting and gardening, the classical music they'd all grown up listening to spilling out of every window and filling the air with a sense of timelessness that Fred loved.

Mac was pleased with the quality of the grapes and said it boded well for the vintage that year. Fred divided her days between learning the ropes of winemaking, helping with the ongoing harvest, and working on the house. The latter was hard work, but rewarding, as the marked wallpaper and chipped woodwork began to disappear, to be replaced by fresh paint, clean curtains, cheap, comfortable furniture, and bright cushions and throws.

Fred enjoyed going into town with Sandi and shopping for knick-knacks to brighten the place up—colorful mobiles with chimes to hang in the windows, paintings of funny blue and red birds called pukekos and the beautiful scarlet flowers of the pohutukawa tree, a set of two large mirrors in the shape of the islands of New Zealand, and metal or porcelain Maori shapes like the *koru*, which was a spiral, or the *hei matau*, which was a stylized fish hook. Sandi was also keen to emphasize her family's history, and bought prints of old paintings of the missionaries arriving at Blue Penguin Bay, showing what the place looked like in the early nineteenth century.

The majority of the money, though, went on the vineyard. In the first few days after the wedding, Fred sat down with Mac at the computer and they went through hundreds of sites looking at vineyard equipment, deciding what was the best way to spend the money they had—what needed to be replaced, versus what they could make do with.

Mac suggested that as they had used hand pickers for so long, they continued to do so for the foreseeable future. Mechanical harvesters, he explained, often had trouble telling the difference between the ripe grapes and any that were moldy, and picked out leaves and stems, or even small animals and bird nests. Instead, they bought a new mechanical crusher and de-stemmer for the red wines, and a new press, the pieces of equipment that Mac said most needed replacing.

After that, they concentrated on replacing or repairing smaller items—new oak barrels, testing equipment, some parts for the filtration machines, and a replacement for the oldest labelling machine.

On Fred's insistence, they also spruced up the workers' rest area, replacing the ancient kitchen with a new sink, microwave, and fridge, throwing away the ripped, stained chairs and wobbly wooden table, and buying a set of comfortable red seats and a new table that would be easier to clean. She also repainted their bathroom and bought new mirrors, hand towels, and other toiletries that made it a more pleasant place for their employees to use.

The days were busy, and Fred spent many of the evenings poring over the books with Mac, trying to make sense of the past few years of accounts, as well as planning for the future. Mac had a keen business mind, and he was full of ideas for where to take the vineyard. But he took great pains to make it clear that she was the one in charge, and all the decisions were ultimately up to her.

The more time she spent with him, the more she began to feel that he was dismantling the steel barriers around her heart piece by piece, and taking down the barbed wire that had surrounded her emotions, keeping him at bay. It wasn't a voluntary thing—she didn't make the decision at any time to forgive him and his family—but she could feel herself softening toward him as he won her over with his calm common sense, his hard work, his dry sense of humor, and the fact that, at all times, he seemed intent on putting her first.

How much of it was to do with the fact that they were married? Fred didn't want to ask him, but she watched him when he was around other women—her sisters, the waitresses in the restaurant, the women who worked on the vineyard—and he was definitely different when he was with her. When he was with other women, he was still funny, still warm, still deferential and gentle and kind, but she noticed that he always kept his hands to himself—she never saw him touch any of them, not even a brush of their arm or a pat on the back.

With herself, though, it felt as if he was always touching her. When he passed her, he would rest a hand on her shoulder. When they were walking through the vineyard and he wanted to attract her attention, he would take her hand and guide her toward him, even though he released it straight afterward. If they were working on the accounts, he'd often sit close enough so that his arm brushed hers, or his knee bumped hers under the table. And sometimes—and this was the oddest thing—if other men were around, in the vineyard or occasionally if they called into town to pick something up, Mac would put a hand in the small of her back, just a touch, light as a feather, but there was something territorial about it. Something possessive. *Mine*, he was saying. *Hands off.*

Fred knew that should annoy her. He was acting as if she was his property. As if she belonged to him, and that went against their agreement that the contract meant nothing to them personally.

Oddly, though, it didn't make her angry. For a start, she was certain he wasn't doing it on purpose—his movements were unthinking, and occasionally he whipped his hand away, as if he'd caught himself doing it.

And secondly, she kind of liked it. Why, she couldn't say. She certainly didn't want him thinking that just because they were married, he had some kind of hold over her, as if he controlled her.

But when he did it, when he touched her, it made her feel less lonely, as if she had someone in her corner, fighting for her against the world.

It seemed ridiculous when she considered his family had almost ruined hers, and he was the last person she should trust. She was healing, there was no doubt about that—the peace of the vineyard and the bay were helping the wounds she'd suffered close over. They would always be there, a subtle ache deep inside, like shrapnel buried beneath the surface, lying dormant until something tweaked it and made it hurt again. She could never forget what James MacDonald had done, and she would never forgive him. But maybe she was close to taking the first steps to forgiving his son.

It was now April. The Chardonnay and Pinot Gris grapes had been harvested, and they were partway through the Merlot and

Chambourcin, with Cabernet grapes being the final ones to be brought in.

One Friday, after the workforce had gone home, Sandi and Ginger declared that they were going into town to grab some dinner and have a few drinks.

Ginger stuck her head around Fred's door. "You coming?"

"Not tonight," Fred replied. "I'm a bit tired. I might have a bath at the house and an early night."

"Boring." Ginger stuck out her tongue. "You're getting old."

"I am. I'm positively ancient. Bugger off."

Ginger laughed. "Have fun with your rubber duck. See you later."

"Don't do anything I wouldn't do," Fred called as the girls left. They just laughed, the door banged, and they were gone.

Fred let out a long sigh. She loved her sisters and luckily they all got on really well, but sometimes she wished she had her own space that consisted of more than just a bedroom. All her life, she'd lived with others, and she'd never had the freedom of a whole house or apartment to herself. Still, she had to count her blessings—there were others who weren't as fortunate as she was, and she had to appreciate what she had.

It had been an odd day. It hadn't rained, but the wind had whipped through the vines, scattering leaves everywhere, and it had left her with a strangely unsettled feeling in her stomach, an awareness of the country moving toward autumn, as if things were on the change.

Refusing to spend the evening musing on the past, she picked up her phone and sent Mac a text.

Is the bathroom free? I fancy a bath.

Her phone beeped.

Yeah, of course.

I'll be up in five, she replied.

She went into the kitchen, took a bottle of Pinot Gris out of the fridge, and poured herself an inch in a glass. Then she went back into her room, sat on the bed, and took the two pieces of paper out of her case. She placed Mac's email aside and spent a few moments reading the letter from her father. Then she laid the paper down and stood to look out at the garden, sipping her wine.

Would Harry be pleased with what his daughters had done here? She hoped he would, even if it had meant she'd gone against his wishes and accessed her inheritance without being properly married.

You *are* properly married, a voice said in her head. Just because she wasn't in love with the guy, it didn't change the legality of that situation—Jackie had been very clear about that.

She sipped her wine, musing on it for a while. Then, when the five minutes had passed, she grabbed a pair of pajamas and headed out of the B&B and up to the house. Russet and gold leaves danced across the path in front of her as she walked, and the cool air held a suggestion of winter to come. One of the websites she'd read in the U.K. had called the Northland the 'winterless north', but Mac had said they still occasionally had frosts in the bay, although rarely any snow.

Thinking of Mac made her feel jittery, and her stomach fluttered. What was wrong with her tonight? She should have brought the bottle of wine with her, but she'd left it in the house. Maybe the soak in the bath would help settle her nerves.

The bathrooms in the B&B had only a shower cubicle, something Sandi thought she might rectify in the future, as she insisted that part of the fun of escaping for a weekend was taking a luxurious bath.

The main house had a surprisingly magnificent bathroom, which unfortunately James had left in a disgusting condition. While Mac had been staying there, he'd used the smaller en suite bathroom that hadn't been in quite such bad condition.

He'd started to get rid of some of the rubbish and the filth in the main one, and Fred had continued the process, cleaning it thoroughly, then giving it a fresh coat of paint. Gradually, she'd returned it to the beautiful room it had once been. It had a huge white sunken bath in front of large sliding glass doors that looked out onto the vineyard, almost making it feel as if you were bathing outside. Fred had no idea why her father would have spent so much on the bathroom, but she thanked him from the bottom of her heart.

Reaching the front door, she knocked, heard Mac's answering hello, and went in.

"You don't have to knock," he said as she walked in. "I keep telling you—it's your house."

"Yeah, well, you might be doing something personal." She stopped in front of the sofa to greet a wagging Scully. Mac was sitting watching the TV, his laptop on his knees, his bare feet propped up on the coffee table.

"Doing something personal? Like what?" he asked, amused.

She shrugged. "You might have had a lady friend here."

"Forsaking all others, Fred. I promised. Sort of. And anyway, you said you'd only be five minutes. I hope I have a bit more stamina and self-control than that." He met her gaze, and his eyes held a touch of mischievousness.

"Maybe you were doing a bit of DIY then. I'd be surprised if that took more than five minutes." Ooh, jeez. She'd only had a tiny glass of wine. Maybe it was because she hadn't eaten.

Mac's eyebrows rose, and his lips curved up. He rested an arm on the back of the sofa, and observed her with interest.

"Did I say that out loud?" Fred said.

"I'm afraid so." Trying not to laugh, he gestured down the corridor with his head. "Enjoy your bath."

"Thanks." She walked past him, face burning. The thought of him carrying out any personal DIY made her all shivery. She could imagine him sitting like he was now, feet planted wide, completely naked, eyes closed and head tipped back while he stroked himself to a climax.

Oh, Fred! Shaking her head, she opened the door and entered the bathroom, desperate to hide her blush.

Then she stopped short. Mac had filled the bath for her, and must have added some of the lavender and peppermint bath salts she'd bought for herself, because the room smelled gorgeous. He'd also placed about a hundred tea lights around the edge of the bath, and he must have been out in the garden, because he'd scattered rose petals in between the candles and on the surface of the water. Vivaldi's Four Seasons was playing on a set of speakers into which he'd set his iPhone, filling the air with the light melody of autumn. And on the shelf beside the bath, he'd placed a glass of Pinot Gris and a saucer holding half a dozen chocolate truffles.

Fred went back out and along the corridor to the living room.

He was studying his laptop, but he looked up when she stopped in front of the sofa.

"Did I forget something?" he said.

She bent down. "You're very sweet," she whispered, and leaned forward and kissed his cheek. "Thank you."

"You deserve it," he said, somewhat gruffly.

"Perhaps I should ask you to get in with me," she said, straightening. "We could play submarines or something."

He met her gaze and held it for a long moment, and her stomach fluttered again.

Finally, he swallowed. "I feel there's a joke somewhere in there about up periscopes," he said, "but I'm damned if I can think of it."

She laughed. He wasn't sure if she was joking, and neither was she, so it was probably best that they both assumed she was.

"I'll see you in a while," she told him. "I'm going to make the most of it."

"Enjoy."

She walked away, feeling his gaze on her, and her lips curved up in a smile.

Chapter Eighteen

While Fred was in the bath, Mac put away his laptop, tidied up a bit, straightened the cushions, then went into the kitchen and leaned against the worktop, arms folded.

He didn't want her to go. He was tired of being on his own, of watching TV and having nobody to talk to. On paper, it sounded like a good idea, but lately when he was alone all he did was think of Fred, and how much he missed her.

"How can we get her to stay?" he asked Scully.

Scully sneezed.

"A good suggestion," he said, "but I need a bit more than that."

He walked out and down the corridor to the bathroom, pausing outside the door. He could hear her singing softly, her high voice mirroring Vivaldi's violins. Smiling, he tapped on the door.

"Yes?" she called.

"I was just wondering… I'm sure you've probably eaten and won't want anything, but just in case, I thought I'd ask…" He was waffling, and he cleared his throat. "You don't fancy dinner, do you? I could knock up some pasta or something." Jeez. Way to make it sound attractive.

There was a slight pause. He looked at his feet and screwed up his nose. He shouldn't have said anything. She was trying to think of a way to refuse him without insulting him.

But to his surprise, she said, "Actually, that would be lovely. I haven't eaten yet. If you don't mind me sitting there in my pajamas."

He laughed. "No worries. I'll get started. No rush though. You take as long as you want."

"Okay, thanks." After a few seconds, she started singing again.

Smiling, he went back into the kitchen and started the dinner.

He was just draining the pasta and mixing it in with the sauce when Fred emerged, her face pink, her hair braided and pinned up on the top of her head, and dressed in the cutest pair of pink pajamas with purple flowers he'd ever seen on a grown woman.

"Don't say anything," she warned him, jumping onto a barstool. "Sandi bought them for me for Christmas and I didn't have the heart to say I'm sure they're for an eight-year-old."

He laughed and brought the pan over to the worktop, dished the pasta into two shallow bowls, added some salad, slid a piece of warmed bread onto the side, and pushed it over to her.

"Thought we might eat in the living room," he said. "Have you seen *Chef's Table*?"

She slid off the stool and picked up her bowl. "No. What's that?"

"A series about head chefs around the world. It's really good." He led the way in to where he'd already placed a couple of glasses of wine on the coffee table. He took the right-hand side of the sofa, and Fred sat on his left. The program had already started, so they began eating while they watched the story of the famous Italian chef unfold.

Mac felt an unusual flood of happiness. His dog lay to his right, while Fred sat only inches away from him, curled up on the sofa. She smelled heavenly, of lavender and mint. Her hair was a little damp around the nape of her neck, and he could imagine her sliding down into the hot water, almost into the bubbles. She looked all soft and curvy in the pajamas, and he was pretty certain she wasn't wearing any underwear. If he were to slide his hands beneath the top, he'd find bare skin, and her breasts would be loose and unrestrained in his hands.

He sighed happily, content to daydream. It was lovely just having someone to watch TV with, to eat with. Fred was easy company—she didn't talk all the time, and she wasn't always asking him what he was thinking or feeling. She didn't goad him or argue with him just for the hell of it, which was something he'd experienced with other women, and disliked intensely. When she did speak, she asked pertinent questions and offered interesting opinions. It was like she spoke his language, and he could count the times he'd been able to say that on the fingers of one hand.

He risked a glance at her, and was surprised to find her looking at him.

"What?" he said.

She shrugged. "Ginger and Sandi have gone out tonight. They asked me if I wanted to go, and I nearly did. I was just thinking that I'm glad I didn't. This is nice. Sitting here, eating dinner, watching TV. With you." Her hazel eyes were bright, clear.

"Like an old married couple," he murmured.

Her lips curved up. "Yeah." She returned her gaze to the bowl in her hands and ate another forkful of pasta. "The sauce is lovely. What's in it?"

"The usual—tomatoes, basil, red wine of course."

"Of course. Have you ever been to Italy?"

"Yes, I went on my OE—that's what the Kiwis call their overseas experience—when I finished uni. I went to England, Spain, France, Italy, and Germany. I already knew then that I wanted to be a viticulturist, so I spent a lot of time at vineyards, discovering how they did things over there. Learnt a lot."

"I haven't travelled much." She watched the views of the Italian countryside on the TV, looking envious. "I've done so little with my life."

It was so unusual for her to say something personal that his eyebrows rose. "I don't think you can say that. Looking after a sick parent can hardly be categorized as having done nothing."

"You know what I mean. My view of the world consists of this." She drew a circle in the air around herself. "I feel very… parochial. I try not to be. I've always read widely, and I try not to be narrow minded, but I'm aware that my experiences are limited."

"You don't strike me that way," he said honestly. "You're like a balloon seller in a city, who occasionally lets go of a balloon and watches it rise into the sky until he can't see it anymore."

She stared at him, and he watched her cheeks slowly turn blush pink. "What an odd thing to say."

"Sorry."

"No… I like it. It's just… nobody's ever said anything like that about me before."

He put his plate on the coffee table, picked up his wine, and turned a little on the sofa toward her. "You've had previous relationships though, right?"

"Yes." She pushed a piece of pasta around the bowl with her fork, then placed the bowl next to his and picked up her wine glass. "A couple. Neither lasted very long, though. I don't know if that was their fault or mine. I knew I'd never be able to leave my mother, and I suppose because of that any effort I put into the relationship was halfhearted. Or maybe it was just because I didn't like them that much." Her lips quirked up, and she sipped her wine.

"You've never been in love?" he asked.

She wiped a mark from the side of the glass. "No." She touched her thumb to her tongue, then scrubbed again. "Have you?"

"There was a girl I met while I was working in Blenheim. Claire. We went out for a few months, then got a place together. It was her idea, and I was twenty-five, twenty-six, I thought it was what I should do, about time I should settle down, you know. I was fond of her. I suppose I loved her."

"What went wrong?"

He shook his head, still puzzled. "I don't know. I guess we drifted apart. She said I wasn't willing to work at the relationship, that I didn't put enough effort in. To this day, I'm not sure what she meant by that. I bought her flowers, took her out to dinner. I didn't leave my socks on the floor. I didn't take her for granted—at least, I didn't think I did. Maybe I did. I don't know."

"Perhaps she meant emotionally," Fred suggested. "She could probably sense that you weren't a hundred percent invested."

"Maybe." He ran a hand through his hair. "She called me a cold fish." Sam had said the same about Fred, he remembered. That made him smile. "She could be right. I know I'm no James Bond—I'm not the kind of guy girls dream about."

Fred's gaze settled on him, holding warmth and… something else he couldn't quite decipher. "How do you know? Not all girls dream about a man who's flamboyant and dynamic. That kind of guy would scare the hell out of me. Some girls like men who are quiet, resourceful, hardworking."

"That makes me sound incredibly dull."

Her eyes met his. "I don't find you dull."

He didn't know what to say to that. Neither did Fred, judging by the way she dropped her gaze.

She put down her wine and picked up the two bowls. "I'll just wash these."

He watched her get up, then rose and followed her out to the kitchen.

She ran some hot water, added the washing up liquid, and began to clean the bowls and the tools he'd used for cooking. Mac would have put them in the dishwasher, but if it meant she was staying for a bit longer, he was happy to let her do it.

He stood next to her, taking the items as she washed them, and drying them with a tea towel. The last rays of the evening sun slanted in through the window across the kitchen. It was growing dark, and he should put the lights on really, but he liked the way the room had turned a deep orange, the new peach-colored walls glowing, the chrome and stainless steel reflecting the sun, as if it was on fire.

The red highlights in Fred's chestnut hair stood out in this light, and he knew that if he released it from its clip and spread it around her shoulders, it would look like beaten copper.

The material of her pajama top gaped a little when she leant forward, treating Mac to an expanse of pale skin and the slight swell of the top of her breasts. It was rude to stare, and he tried to tear his gaze away, but he couldn't. The curve of her neck, the rounded blush of her cheeks, the shell of her ear, they all fascinated him, and he had to fight not to bend his head and press his lips to them.

He felt as if the passion and fire of his youth had subsided into barely glowing embers over the last few years, and he'd been content to let the glow fade, conscious that he would never set the world alight, and happy enough to exist in his corner of the world. But when Fred had arrived, it was as if she'd fanned those embers, causing the fire in his belly to leap into life again. He hadn't felt this slow burn, this ache deep inside him, for a long time, and it had taken him by surprise. He wanted this woman, wanted her badly, and he didn't know how he was going to cope with being around her, with seeing her every day, if he wasn't able to touch her.

Fred was holding the saucepan he'd cooked the pasta in, but she lowered it into the water and stood there for a second, looking at it. He paused in the act of drying a bowl, wondering what was wrong. She lifted her hands out of the water, holding them up and examining how the suds had turned orange in the evening light, sparkling and shimmering, like fish scales.

She turned toward him and looked up. Her lips parted. And then she lifted her arms around his neck, leaned against him, and pressed her lips to his.

Mac was so shocked that for a second he just stood there. Her wet, warm hands splayed into his hair, and her soft body molded to his. Was this really happening? His brain refused to work—he was afraid he'd misread the signs, that she was just saying thank you or something, and that if he touched her, she'd pull back with a start.

Then she moved her head back a few inches, and looked into his eyes. Her own were half-lidded and sultry, her lips bare and dry.

"Want me to stop?" she whispered. She wasn't just saying thank you. She really wanted him.

Mac's lips curved up, and joy flooded through him.

He put his hands on her hips and turned her so her butt rested against the sink. Stepping closer, until their bodies were flush, he pressed against her from her breasts to her thighs. He studied her face, thinking how beautiful she was, and how much he loved the way she hadn't even stopped to dry her hands.

Then he lowered his head and kissed her.

She murmured her approval, clutching her fingers in his hair, and Mac sighed and gave himself over to the kiss. He felt as if he was kissing a piece of autumn, bathed in the evening glow, tasting the apple and pear from the wine she'd had, his nose filling with the smell of lavender and mint. She opened her mouth to his tongue, and he dipped it inside, fireworks going off from the roots of his hair and travelling all the way through his body to his feet. He slid his hands around her waist, still over the top of her pajamas, loving the way she was so soft, with none of the elastic and wire of women's underwear that constrained and tightened and pushed a woman's natural figure out of shape.

He skimmed his hands up her ribs, then behind to feel her narrow back and the angles of her shoulder blades, then over her shoulders and down under her arms, until finally he brushed across her breasts. She didn't complain, just sighed and arched her back a little, so he cupped her breasts and ran his thumbs across her nipples. She was so soft—her breasts felt like ripe fruit in his palms, and he groaned as her nipples tightened and hardened, responding to his touch.

Finally, he moved his hands down her back and beneath the loose elastic of her pajama bottoms, sliding his hands over the muscles of her bottom, and pulled her against him, pressing his erection against her soft mound. God, but he wanted her. He'd take her, right here, right now, if he could, strip her naked here in the kitchen, and let the rays of the late sun pour hot gold over her skin, making love to her until she clenched her hands in his hair and cried out his name.

"Yes," she whispered, nibbling his bottom lip, and he knew that once again she'd read his mind, had seen what he was thinking, and wanted it too.

"Here?" he mumbled. Surely she deserved to be in a soft bed, to be kissed and touched for hours, to be worshipped.

But she just nodded, grabbed the bottom of his T-shirt, and pulled it up and over his head. His heart swelled. Was there anything as wonderful in the world as being wanted?

Chapter Nineteen

Everything had fled Fred's mind except how it felt to have this man kissing her, holding her, looking at her with such desire that it was setting her alight. Nothing else mattered. Not the vineyard, not their fake marriage, not Ginger or Sandi or her father or James MacDonald. She didn't want to think about the past or the future, or consequences, or the problems this might cause. For once in her life, she wanted to be a slave to her senses, to concentrate only on what her heart wanted, what her body craved.

She dropped Mac's T-shirt to the floor and rested her palms on his chest. She could tell he wasn't afraid of hard work—as far as she knew, he didn't go to the gym, but his muscles were hard and defined, and there wasn't an ounce of fat on him. She'd never been with a man like this. The two guys she'd dated in the past had been boys in comparison, arrogant and eager to screw her body but not caring about her mind, as alien to her as the celebrities she saw in the magazines and on TV.

But this… this was a real man. He smelled of the outdoors, of mown grass, leather, the rich smell of earth, warmed by the sun. The way he described himself made him sound inexperienced and at a loss with women, but she could tell from how he was touching her, the sure slide of his hands over her body, that he knew how to pleasure a girl. This was no fumbling eighteen-year-old, not even a cocky post-grad—this was a man, with a man's desires, and Fred shivered from the sheer anticipation of making love with him.

She'd sensed that he was inches away from taking her there and then, on the kitchen worktop, and her pulse had raced at the thought. She wanted to get carried away by passion, to be impulsive for once in her life. She didn't want to think about what she should or ought to do. *Just take me*, she wanted to beg, and even though she didn't have the courage to voice the words, she knew that he heard them, because his hands were gentle but firm, his kisses demanding rather than asking.

He lifted her pajama top, and Fred closed her eyes as he pulled it over her head and dropped it to the floor. She stood semi-naked in the kitchen, conscious of the window looking out onto the vineyard and hoping none of the grape pickers had stayed behind hoping for some overtime. She could feel the warmth of the evening sun on her skin, but it didn't come close to the heat of his gaze.

"You're so beautiful," he whispered, and she opened her eyes and looked up at him, holding her breath at his awed desire. He cupped her breast and stroked the tip with his thumb, and she looked down and watched the nipple peak, felt the answering shudder reverberate right through her, like a tuning fork tapped on the side of the piano.

"Mmm." She tipped back her head, and then she felt his hands on her hair, removing the clip so the braid unfurled down over her shoulder. He pulled out the band at the end, and then his fingers were parting the strands, unravelling them until they tumbled down her body in a sheet of silk.

"I knew it would be soft," he said hoarsely, lifting a section to his nose and inhaling.

Dropping her hair, he kissed her mouth, then up her cheekbone to her ear. His lips trailed down her neck, along her shoulder, then over her breastbone, and Fred inhaled as he bent and closed his mouth over a nipple.

God, it felt good, and she leaned back on the worktop, arching her back to push the nipple into his mouth. He sucked, just hard enough, and she cried out, her body humming.

His tongue washed over to her other nipple, lips tugging, mouth sucking, and Fred tipped her head right back, feeling her hair coiling on the rimu worktop. Mac leaned on her, his weight pressing into her—she could feel the hard length of his erection even through his jeans, eager for her, desperate to bury itself in her warmth.

Again, she felt his hands at the top of her pajama bottoms, but this time he tugged them down her legs, and she stepped out of them. Standing before him naked, she caught her breath as he raked her with his gaze, skimming down her waist and over her belly before lingering at the top of her thighs.

Fred ached for him. Now she'd made the decision to sleep with him, she couldn't wait any longer. "Condom?" she asked, hoping beyond hope that he wouldn't give her a blank look.

His eyebrows rose, then he patted his jeans pockets before looking around, presumably searching for his wallet.

"Coffee table?" she suggested.

He walked into the living room, past Scully, who lay with her nose on her paws, apparently bored with the show, and returned triumphant, opening his wallet. Flipping out a foil wrapper, he tossed the wallet aside and came back to her.

She lifted herself up on the worktop, parted her knees, and pulled him toward her.

"You're sure?" he murmured.

She nodded and fumbled at the top of his jeans. He didn't need telling twice. He unbuttoned them, slid the zipper, and pushed down his boxers.

Fred watched, heart racing, as he rolled on the condom. Her mouth had gone dry. It had been a long time since she'd done this, and he wasn't a small man.

To her surprise, he slid a finger beneath her chin and lifted it so she looked into his eyes. He smiled, and it was a lazy smile, a lusty one, that told her he knew what he was doing, and he was going to take his time, so all she had to do was enjoy it. She let him kiss her, opening her mouth to him, and at the same time felt his warm hand on her thigh. His thumb slid down, stroking between her legs, parting her folds, and she moaned as it found her clit and circled over it, smoothing her moisture through her swollen skin.

"Mac," she whispered, trying to stop her hips rocking against the movement of his thumb.

"Mmm." He dipped down again, retrieving more moisture, and she sighed, dropping back onto her elbows.

Unfortunately, as she did so, she knocked against the tap, and cold water splashed into the sink, throwing a shower of droplets over her naked skin. Before she could lift a hand to turn the tap off, Mac cupped a hand beneath the cool water, scooped it up, and tossed it over her body.

She squealed, and he laughed, then bent and covered her taut nipple with his mouth again. Fred groaned and opened her legs wider, and he caught another handful of water, this time letting it trickle over her belly and down her thighs. The coolness contrasted with the heat of her skin, and she felt her muscles tighten inside, almost coming on the spot.

"Please," she begged, and he took the hint and guided his erection to her entrance.

"Take a breath," he said. Puzzled, she did so. "Now breathe out," he instructed. "Slowly." As she blew out the breath, he pushed forward.

She gasped and clenched, and he stopped, withdrew, then pushed again. Gradually, he slid inside her, half an inch more each time until his hips met the back of her thighs and he was up to the hilt.

Fred closed her eyes, reveling in the feel of him, hot, hard, throbbing, deep within. She'd forgotten how amazing it felt to have a man inside her, to have his hands holding her tight, his lips on her body. He scooped up more water and splashed it over her, then followed it with his tongue, and she moaned and wrapped her legs around his waist.

"Jesus," he said, and he began to move, sliding in and out of her swollen flesh and teasing her more toward the edge with every thrust.

"Oh, Mac…" Her eyelids fluttered open a fraction, and she looked up into his that burned like a blue flame, so intense she thought she might self-combust.

He leaned forward over her, the angle meaning that he ground against her with each movement of his hips, and Fred's breaths grew erratic as pleasure spiraled. She couldn't believe she was doing this, lying in the late sunshine, stark naked, a gorgeous man thrusting her to oblivion, with the blinds still open so that anyone could see them should they happen to walk by. But she didn't care, couldn't think about anything except his mouth and his hands and his hot hardness inside her, and all her muscles were tensing, and she cried out, her orgasm bursting through her, sharp as the first bite into a chili, and just as powerful.

Mac thrust harder, filling the air with the slick sounds of their lovemaking, and then he shuddered and groaned. Fred lifted her head to watch the pleasure spread across his face as his climax took him, as strong and powerful as her own, by the look of it. His hands were tight on her thighs, his body hard as rock, turned brick-red in the setting sun, the color of Merlot. He was magnificent, and her heart thundered at the realization of what they'd done. They'd consummated their marriage, and even though she told herself it mattered not a jot, because it was just a piece of paper, in her heart she knew that was very far from the truth.

His eyelids fluttered open, and he focused on her. "Wow," he said.

She reached over and turned off the tap. "I'm all wet," she complained.

"My work here is done."

She laughed and tipped up her face as he leaned over her to press his lips to hers. They exchanged a long, sweet kiss, and it was with some reluctance that she watched him straighten.

"Careful," he said, and withdrew from her, holding the condom until he was free and could dispose of it. Fred sighed, already missing him, expecting him to walk off and get a drink from the fridge or something. But he came straight back to her and, to her surprise, lifted her easily into his arms.

Without saying anything else, he walked out of the kitchen and along the corridor to the main bedroom, carried her over to the bed, and lowered her down.

"I shouldn't stay," she protested. "Ginger and Sandi will be back."

"They'll be a while yet." He stretched out beside her, all hard muscles and tanned skin. "Come here." He held out his arms.

There was nothing wrong with taking a few minutes to relax against that glorious body. The pace of her heart began to slow, and she sighed and snuggled up against him. Beside the bed, she heard Scully sigh as she lay.

"That was nice." He tucked one arm under his head and used the fingers of the other to play with Fred's hair.

"Mmm." She rested her chin on his chest and looked up at him. "Did I shock you?"

"A bit." He smiled, telling her that he didn't mind.

"Sorry about that."

"Don't apologize. It was a good sort of shock."

"I guess it's not quite how you expected the evening to end."

He gave a lazy shrug. "A man can dream."

He'd been dreaming about going to bed with her? It was nice to know he hadn't just taken advantage of her offer.

She yawned. "I feel all loose and floppy, like a chicken breast beaten with a mallet."

"Mmm." His fingers continued to run through her hair, a soothing gesture that made her eyes start to close. She shouldn't stay here. She didn't want the girls to come back and find her bed empty.

This was nobody else's business, and she didn't want them making fun of her, or trying to push her into admitting that their marriage was anything more than a signed document.

Just a few more minutes, she told herself. Then she'd kiss him goodbye and leave, and that would be that.

*

The room grew dark and cool, and Fred felt as if someone had given her a sleeping drug. Her limbs were heavy and refused to do as she bid. Several times, she tried to rise, but each time Mac's arm felt like an iron band around her waist, holding her there.

The shadows lengthened and the moon rose in the sky, and still she couldn't move, couldn't speak, could only lie there, feeling the race of her heart, listening to the moreporks calling in the trees. She glanced at the clock—it was nearly midnight. Midnight! She hadn't meant to sleep for so long. Still, though, she couldn't bring herself to move.

It was only gradually that she became aware of a shape in the corner of the room. She blinked rapidly, trying to clear her vision, but she still couldn't make it out. It was just a shadow, surely… But after a few minutes, it began to take shape. It was a figure. A man. He stood in the semi-darkness, still and menacing. The moonlight sliced across the bed like a steel blade, moving toward the corner as the moon rose. She watched the silver bar start at his feet and lift up his body like a laser scanning a barcode, up and up, illuminating as it went. Eventually, it reached his face. A straight nose cast a shadow over a wide mouth. His gray hair shone dully in the light. His hazel eyes looked like flat, lifeless discs. Familiar eyes, and yet they weren't filled with love. They were angry, accusatory, and although he didn't move, didn't say anything, fear and panic rushed through her, and she gave a great gasp and sat bolt upright, her heart pounding.

Chapter Twenty

Mac snapped awake as the woman in his arms suddenly sat upright with a gasp.

He'd fallen asleep—he hadn't meant to. Maybe an hour had passed—the last of the sun's rays had vanished, and the room had subsided into semi-darkness.

Fred had scrabbled up the bed until her back reached the headboard, and now she sat staring at the corner of the room, her chest heaving, clearly terrified.

"Sweetheart, what is it?" He couldn't see anything there.

"There was…" She swallowed hard. "Someone standing there."

He glanced over. "Nobody's there, honey."

"There was…"

"Fred, Scully would have barked if someone had come into the room."

Her gaze flicked to him, and he could see the white of her eyes around her irises. "Are you sure?"

His brow furrowed. He leaned over to the bedside table and switched on a lamp, casting the room in a warm glow. Scully lay by the side of the bed, her head on her paws, although she stood as he rose. He pulled on a pair of track pants. She looked unconcerned—there had been nobody there, not even someone she knew, because she would have been excited to see them.

He suspected that Fred had been dreaming, but nevertheless he clicked his fingers at Scully and got her to follow him around the room, then walked out along the corridor and did a quick patrol of the house. Scully sniffed happily, spotting nothing. It was true that he hadn't locked the front door, but she ran out and did a pee, and showed no signs of suspicion that anyone had passed by that way.

Eventually, he returned to the bedroom with her. Fred still sat against the headboard, clutching the duvet, her shoulders drawn up like a little girl, and her gaze still fixed on the corner of the room.

"It's all right." He sat on the bed. "Scully didn't spot anything."

Her eyes slowly came to meet his, and gradually her shoulders relaxed. "It was just a dream."

"I think so. Probably."

She moistened her lips. "Thank you for taking me seriously, though."

"No worries. Who did you think you saw?"

"My father." She rubbed her nose. "It was a dream, of course it was. It was darker in here—I looked at the clock in the dream and it said midnight, and it's only eight."

"Did he say something?"

"No. He just stared at me. But he was really angry." Her face shone pale as the moon, and when he reached over and rested a hand on her arm, her skin felt cold and clammy.

"Why don't you come into the kitchen? I'll make us a cup of tea." Without waiting for her to reply, he went out and fetched her pajamas and brought them back, then left her to get dressed while he returned to the kitchen and filled the kettle. It had just reached the boil when she appeared. She looked younger in the pajamas, with her hair loose around her shoulders, and he felt a surge of protectiveness and pity for this young woman who'd been through so much.

"Come on." He knew she liked Earl Grey, and he made the tea, then carried their mugs into the living room and pulled her down onto the sofa beside him. "The girls aren't back yet," he told her. "The car's still missing."

She sipped the tea. To his relief, a touch of color had returned to her cheeks. Scully rested her snout on Fred's knee, and Fred stroked her ear.

"I'm sorry you had a bad dream," he said. "I hope I wasn't the cause of it."

"Of course not. At least, not directly." She ran a finger around the rim of the mug. "I guess what you said was playing on my mind—what my father might say about the two of us getting married. I can't help but believe he'd be angry with me. I didn't really think it through. I just wanted the money. But now, I keep thinking about what James did, and how angry Dad would be with me for going against his wishes, especially with James's son. And I guess after what we just did..." She looked into her tea.

Mac's spirits sank. The last thing he wanted was for her to feel guilty or upset because they'd slept together. "I'm sure he wouldn't feel like that. I'm convinced that if he'd known what my dad was going to do, he wouldn't have placed that clause on your inheritance the way he did. I can't believe he'd be angry with you for trying to do your best. Or with me, as it happens. I liked Harry, and I'm sure he liked me too. He would be pleased I'm looking out for you. I hope he would, anyway."

"Hope... that's all we can do, isn't it?" She looked somewhat forlorn. Then she gave a little laugh and flicked him a wry look. "I'm so sorry—this isn't the best post-coital discussion, is it?"

He smiled and reached out to hold her hand. "Hey, I'm just glad you stayed for a while. We might not have gone into this with the intention of it developing into something, but that doesn't mean we don't have feelings for each other. We're friends, aren't we?"

She gave a cautious nod.

"Good," he said. "Look, I know you have your sisters, but you're the oldest, and I can see that you feel responsibility to be the strong one. I doubt that you open up to them often."

She wrinkled her nose at him. "Not much, no."

"Then I hope you feel as if you can talk to me."

She turned her mug in her hands. "We agreed that the marriage didn't mean anything. I don't want you to feel as if you have to sit and listen to my woes just because we signed a bit of paper."

He felt a flare of impatience. Why couldn't she trust him? "Give me some credit, will you? I like you, Fred. Come on, talk to me. I can see you're struggling. You've been through a hell of a hard time. I've been waiting for you to open up, to tell me about your mother, but you seem determined to keep everything to yourself. Isn't a problem shared a problem halved?"

She tipped her head from side to side. "Maybe, but I suppose I'm also scared of giving voice to my fears in case it makes them real."

"I don't believe that. Do you?"

"Okay, maybe not, but sometimes talking about things stirs it all up again, like picking at a scab and stopping it healing."

"And not talking about it leaves it festering, like refusing to clean out a wound."

She poked her tongue out at him. "Stop using my own metaphors on me."

"I just want to understand you. To get to know you better."

"Mac, what we just did..."

"Are you going to give me a lecture about how it meant nothing, and I mustn't get my hopes up?"

Now she was getting exasperated. "Something like that."

"Save your words. I get it. I'm not assuming that because we slept together it'll happen again." Although he hoped it would. "I like you. It's as simple as that. I wanted to help—I still do."

She scratched at a mark on her pajama bottoms. "I suppose I have trouble believing you're doing this out of the kindness of your heart."

"Well, believe it, baby. I really am that great a person."

She laughed. "Okay."

"Come on. Tell me about your mum."

Immediately, her smile vanished. "I don't want to talk about her."

Jeez, it was like getting blood out of a really, really hard stone. He should give up, but he couldn't. He gave a huff of frustration.

"I'm sorry," she whispered. "It's just..." She bit her lip. "I like the way you look at me, and I don't want that to change."

He frowned, puzzled. "Why would I look at you differently?"

She studied her hands, and suddenly he understood. She was ashamed.

"Fred," he murmured. "Nothing you could tell me would make me think any less of you. I'm not judgmental—at least, I try not to be. Everything has a context, and I know you've had a hard time. Tell me about it."

She swallowed, and for a moment he thought she wasn't going to say anything.

Then she sighed, obviously deciding it was time to confess. "I told you Mum was bipolar."

"Yes."

"Her illness grew worse as time went by. Sometimes, she was okay, but the bad episodes became more frequent and intense. After Dad left, I looked after her. I taught myself to touch type and took secretarial courses in the evenings. I temped a lot—it suited me, as I could do a few days here and there and not have to commit to a full-time job, because when she was bad, she needed me at home. It was hard, but I loved her, and I knew it wasn't her fault. Her husband had abandoned her, and even though she'd cheated on him, I knew she loved him. I felt sorry for her." Her lips pressed into a thin line.

"What happened?"

"Dad died," Fred said simply. "And our solicitor forwarded your email. I sat there for ages, reading his letter over and over. I couldn't believe it. All those years I'd spent hating him, and it wasn't his fault, or at least, not only his fault."

"What did you do?"

She gazed into the distance, and he had a feeling she wasn't seeing the living room window or the view outside, but instead some other time and place. "I confronted her. She admitted destroying his and my letters. She told me she was worried he'd take us all away and she'd lose us all. She cried and begged my forgiveness."

Mac knew they were drawing near to the heart of the matter, and he felt like holding his breath.

She frowned. "I was horrified to know he'd died thinking we didn't love him and wanted nothing to do with him."

"I get that," he said.

She turned her shining hazel eyes to him. "You have to understand what kind of daughter I was up until that point. I never rebelled. Never argued or shouted. Never challenged my mother. Ginger and Sandi both dyed their hair, had tantrums, did all the things you should do as a teen, but I never did. I always did what I was told—I was always polite and deferential, the perfect daughter. Until that day."

Mac put down his mug. "What happened?"

"I lost it. I screamed at her that she'd ruined my life. I felt so utterly devastated. She was my mother—she was supposed to support me, be there for me, and instead she'd been cruel and selfish. She'd let me throw my own life away, and she'd ruined my relationship with my father."

He went cold inside. What was she trying to tell him? She hadn't turned physical toward her mother, surely? God, please no. Don't let her tell him that.

But she continued, "I walked out, the first time I'd ever done that. I drove down to the sea and spent hours walking along the sea wall, so miserable, absolutely heartbroken. I thought about throwing myself in. Came very close to it. But for the first time, I felt a seed of determination inside me. I wasn't going to let her ruin my life anymore. I was done with someone else controlling me. I decided I was going to move out, maybe go to nursing school, start all over again…"

Her voice trailed off. She fell silent for a moment. He didn't dare say anything to break the spell.

Then she blinked and swallowed. "When I got back…" She was trembling now. "When I walked in, I saw her on the sofa. A bottle of pills lay on its side, a couple of them on the floor. She'd taken an overdose."

All his tension left him in a rush. "Ah, Fred…"

"I rang for an ambulance immediately, and they took her to hospital, but I was too late. The pills had done too much damage, and she died the next day." She stared at him, white-faced. She looked terrified of his reaction.

"Sweetheart," he said. "It wasn't your fault."

As if someone had broken the wall of a dam, the tears tumbled down her cheeks, and she put her face in her hands.

He slid an arm around her. She stiffened, but he tugged her and said, "Come here," and she turned to him and pressed her face to his bare chest. Gradually, he felt her melt against him as she let go of the last dregs of resistance.

Mac whispered, "Shhh," and stroked her back. "It's okay," he murmured, over and over again, while outside the rain began to fall lightly, pattering against the windows.

It was a long time before she sat back. "I'm sorry," she whispered, tugging a tissue from a pocket in her pajama top to wipe her eyes.

"It's okay." He kept his arm around her. "I'm glad you told me. Jeez, you girls have had a tough time."

"Yeah, I suppose we have. Ginger and Sandi took it hard, but of course they weren't there when it happened. I couldn't help but blame myself. If I hadn't shouted at her… if I'd reacted better when I found out what she'd done… she'd still be here."

"You don't know that," he said. "The guilt would probably still have been too much for her. She was ill, honey, she had a disease that meant she was always going to overreact, and there was nothing you could do about that. You did an amazing job looking after her for all those years. You shouldn't be too hard on yourself."

She let out a shaky sigh. "We sold the house. Because she took her own life and had a mental illness that she didn't disclose when she took out the policy, the insurance wouldn't pay out, so the proceeds of the house sale went to paying off the mortgage and the credit card bills she left behind. But at least we're shot of it. I don't want to live there and neither do Ginger or Sandi."

"Now I can see why you wanted a fresh start."

"Mmm." She pulled up her knees, wrapped her arms around them, and laid her cheek on them. "I wish I could have known my father. I can't remember him well, so it's hard to know what his reaction would have been to what's happened. It hurts to think of him dying here alone. He trusted your father, and it's horrible to think of James turning on him like that. I can only imagine how that would have hurt him, if he'd been aware of it."

As always, Mac felt a deep, dark burn of resentment at the remembrance of what his father had done. "Yeah."

"Our lives could have been so different," she whispered. "I'll never forgive James."

She met his gaze, and his spirits sank. She hated his father, and he couldn't blame her, because he did too. He wished he could wave a wand and make James MacDonald not be his father. But he couldn't. He was stuck with him, with his blood, his genes, and he would never be able to change it.

And Fred knew that. He would always be James's son in her eyes. She would never be able to look at him without remembering what his father had done to hers, and how their lives had been ruined. She would never be able to put that aside and love him the way a real wife would her husband. His dreams were futile, written on rice paper to be torn into tiny pieces that would float away on the wind like confetti.

Chapter Twenty-One

Fred tried to put what happened that night to the back of her mind.

It wasn't easy. She and Mac were spending a lot of time together working on the vineyard, and it seemed as if every time she turned around, he was working with his shirt off, looking all muscly and shiny and manly, distracting her from whatever she was doing.

Half of her wondered if he was doing it on purpose—he must know he had this effect on her, after what happened in the house that night. But the other half knew it wasn't intentional. Mac was kind, polite, and nice to her, but he was a tad distant, born, she knew, from the fact that she'd said she could never forgive his father for what he'd done.

She wished she could take that back now. She'd meant it at the time—she still meant it—but she wished she hadn't said it to Mac. What his father had done had angered him, but James was still his father, and she knew more than anyone how you could hate someone for what they'd done but want to defend them at the same time.

She shouldn't have slept with him. It had been a monumental mistake, a moment of weakness on her part. He wasn't her enemy, not at all—she wasn't foolish enough to tell herself that. He'd done everything he could to offset his father's cruel actions. But he was still a MacDonald. And far from banishing her bad dreams, it only made them worse. She got them every night now, and they were always the same. She'd wake, or dreaming she was waking, and there would be a sinister figure standing in the corner of her room. Sometimes it was her mother, sometimes her father, but they were always menacing, filled with disapproval and anger. She'd wake for real then, her heart pounding, covered with sweat, and more often than not she'd end up in tears. She had no idea how to banish these phantoms. She'd moved across the world, done her best to get the vineyard back on its feet. What did she have to do to move on?

SERENITY WOODS

The harvest continued. The Merlot grapes were all brought in, and they started on the Cabernet. It was hard work, but Fred was learning so much. She could now tell just by looking which grapes were ready and which weren't, and her palate was becoming more discerning. A few times a week, she, Ginger, and Sandi would treat themselves to a bottle of wine or two from the supermarket, and they'd compare these to their own, gradually developing a nose for the different notes until they could not only tell a Merlot from a Cabernet, and a Pinot Gris from a Chardonnay, but they could pick out the individual notes, and they finally began to understand when different casks had been used, or how strong the tannins were.

These evenings together became precious, because all three of them were working hard throughout the day. Ginger had spent a lot of time in Russell talking to suppliers and fishermen, sourcing local produce, and was starting to serve her new platters, which were already gaining praise on Northland tourist websites. Sandi had finished decorating two of the four bedrooms in the B&B, and had transformed a good part of the garden, which now looked like a tropical paradise rather than an Amazonian jungle. They all loved their work, but it was with some relief that they met up in the evenings, to discuss what they'd done that day, and also to relax.

"Mac doesn't join us anymore," Ginger said one evening when they were halfway through a bottle of Sauvignon. "I miss him."

"He's around all day every day," Fred pointed out. But her sister was right. He no longer came in with them in the evenings. He'd withdrawn from them, and that was her fault.

"He was loading his car up with boxes," Sandi said, flipping through a magazine. "Is he moving out of the house, Fred?"

She looked at Sandi, startled. "When was this?"

"When I came in." Sandi flicked her gaze up and raised an eyebrow. "I thought he'd said he'd move to Russell with his mother for a while so you could have the house."

"So *we* could have it," Fred corrected absently. "Yes, he did, but I didn't think he'd be going yet…"

"Well I'm happy to stay in the B&B flat," Sandi said. "It's self-contained, and it makes sense for me to be here on call in case any of the visitors were to want anything after hours. What about you, are you moving up there?" She looked at Ginger.

Ginger shrugged. "Don't know. I was thinking about getting a place in Russell. I have my eye on a cottage that's been advertised for rent. It's tiny, but it's all I'd need, and every morning I'd be able to get up and have a walk along the beach and meet the fishermen. I'd have first pick of all the catches. So I'm quite happy for you to have the house, Fred."

"It's too big just for me," Fred pointed out.

"Maybe you should ask Mac to stay, then," Sandi said mischievously.

Fred stared at her, feeling the blood drain from her face.

"Hey, what did I say?" Sandi leaned forward in alarm.

"Nothing..." Fred swallowed hard.

"Told you," Ginger said to Sandi.

Sandi frowned and gave Fred a curious look. "Have you two... you know? Slept together?"

All the blood returned to Fred's face in a rush, and her cheeks burned. "No, of course not. Well, maybe. All right, yes. But it was only the once." She leaned her elbows on the table and buried her face in her hands. "Please, don't chide me."

"Chide you?" Sandi laughed, and Ginger snorted.

"You're married," Ginger pointed out. "It's perfectly legal."

"Oh, don't." Fred dipped her head and sank her hands into her hair. "I shouldn't have. I feel terrible."

"Why?"

"Because he's James MacDonald's son," Fred snapped.

"Yes," Sandi said, "his son. He's not James himself. I might have something to say about you sleeping with James."

"Especially because he's dead," Ginger added.

Fred dropped her hands and glared at them both. Anger seared through her. Why didn't they understand? "This isn't a laughing matter. All I can think about is how angry Dad would be with me. Not only have I gone against his wishes and married to get his money, I married the son of the man who pretended to be his friend and then betrayed him. Don't you think we all carry some responsibility for our family's deeds?"

"You've got your own Greek play going on right there, haven't you?" Ginger said.

"Don't make fun of me."

"I'm not, Fred, but you have to lighten up a little. There's this gorgeous guy who's really into you—do you think you should pass up the chance of a little happiness because of what his dad did to our dad?"

"I can't forget it," Fred said simply.

"Do you blame Mac for what his father did?" Sandi asked.

"I know it wasn't his fault. But I don't know if I can put it aside." She closed her eyes, and immediately she could see the figure standing in the corner of the room, disapproving, angry. She opened her eyes again, suddenly tired. "It's my guilt playing on my mind. I can't get rid of it, and until I do, I don't think I could ever be with Mac, not in that way."

"But it's pointless guilt," Ginger said, obviously frustrated. "I understand why you blame yourself for what happened to Mum—even though I don't agree that any of it was your fault—but Mum burning Dad's letters, and Dad dying thinking we didn't want anything to do with him—that was out of your control and you're not to blame for that." Her cheeks had flushed—they were all getting emotional now.

"I know." Fred attempted to speak calmly. "But guilt's not rational, is it? The 'what ifs' and 'I should haves' keep playing on a loop in my head. I should have guessed that Mum would try to stop our communication, but I always try to think the best of people, and I refused to believe she would be that nasty. But what if I'd made more of an effort to contact Dad, emailed or phoned? If we'd been in touch, I'd have known about the will, and James wouldn't have been able to fake another one. I probably wouldn't have flown off the handle at Mum, and she'd... she'd still be here."

"But she's not," Ginger said, "and you know what? I'm relieved."

"Ginger!" Sandi looked horrified.

"What?" Ginger lifted her chin. "I'm just saying what we're all thinking, except that you two won't admit it. I loved Mum, of course I did, with all my heart, and I wish she hadn't died, but she did, and I'm sad, but I'm also relieved. And I wasn't even the one who looked after her all the time. It must be a relief for you, too, Fred? Not to have that responsibility?"

"I can't... Don't make me say that," Fred whispered.

"Stop it," Sandi scolded Ginger. "How can you be so bloody cruel?"

"I'm not being cruel." Ginger looked suddenly tearful. "Fred's blaming herself for everything, and it's not right. Mum died because she had an illness, a horrible, fucking awful disease that had sunk its claws into her brain and eaten away at it until it possessed her, like a demon. People argue—they shout at each other and blame each other for things when they're angry, it happens all the time. But normal people don't then go and kill themselves after an argument. I don't know whether it was the sickness that did it, or whether it was just her nature, but not telling us about Dad's letters was a nasty thing to do. She killed herself because the guilt was too much for her, not because you shouted at her."

Sandi had gone pale, but she turned thoughtful eyes to her sister. "She's right, Fred. It wasn't your fault."

"I know. I know." Fred covered her face with her hands again. "Of course I know that. But I can't shake this feeling that both of them are watching me. I keep dreaming about them, and they're always angry and disapproving."

"They're not." Sandi took her hand. "If they were here, they'd be thrilled with what you've done, not angry."

"Would they? You don't know that." Fred withdrew her hand and stood. "I know you both mean well, and I'm sorry to be such trouble. I wish I could just put everything aside and start again. I thought I could—that's why I came here, but I'm beginning to realize I can't do that. You bring your emotional baggage with you, unfortunately, stowed in the hold of the plane with all your bags. It's not going to go away. I guess I'm just going to have to live with it."

She tucked her chair under the table, turned, and left the room.

Outside, the early evening air was dry and cool, although clouds bunched on the horizon, promising rain. In the nearby orchards, the feijoas and kiwifruit were ready for harvest, while the mandarins were ripening into tiny round suns.

Her hands in the pockets of her jeans, she walked through the garden, out of the gate, and across the path toward the house. Sure enough, Mac's ute stood outside, filled with boxes, and he was in the process of stuffing a sports bag in a gap.

She stopped beside him. "Going somewhere?"

He paused, not looking at her, and pushed harder to get the sports bag in. "Thought it was about time I moved out."

Scully ran up to her, and Fred dropped to her haunches to bury her hands and nose into the dog's fur. "You don't have to," she mumbled, feeling the dog's rough tongue wash over her face.

"I do." He placed another bag on the passenger seat and shut the door. "This is your house, yours and Sandi's and Ginger's. It's time to put things in their rightful place and move on." He turned on his heel and walked off, back into the house.

Fred pushed to her feet and followed him slowly. She felt miserable, so miserable she could barely drag herself up the path.

In the living room, she stood and watched him packing a final box with DVDs, magazines, and other bits and pieces he'd gathered up. The house looked bare, and it was only now that she realized how much she liked him being there.

She stood by the sofa, her shoulders hunched. He thrust a couple of old paperbacks in the box; one of them caught on the edge and tore, but he just jammed it in. He was angry.

"Mac…"

He shook his head, but didn't say anything, just continued to pack. Scully lay by the front door, her snout on her paws, picking up on their mood.

Mac was wearing tight jeans and an All Blacks shirt that clung to his torso. He was a fine figure of a man, beautifully sculpted—she could remember how those muscles had felt beneath her fingers, how thick his hair was. It had felt so good when he was inside her, holding her so tightly, kissing her with just the right amount of force to make her quiver. She longed to experience that again, yearned with all her heart.

He glanced up then, looked at her face, and his brows drew together. "Don't," he said hoarsely, tearing his gaze away. "Don't look at me like that."

A tear ran down her face. "Don't go."

His hands tightened on the edges of the box. "How can I stay, Fred? It's killing me being so near you all day every day and not being able to touch you."

Her jaw dropped. "Are you leaving the vineyard? Leaving the job as well?"

He glared at the contents of the box. "I don't know. I just know I have to get out of here, because otherwise I'm going to spend every evening staring at the door, hoping you'll come in for a bath… I keep dreaming about those fucking pajamas. You were so soft in them, so beautiful…" His gaze came back to her face, and he looked helpless, lost.

She moistened her lips. "I'm sorry."

"Don't apologize!" His eyes blazed. "Not everything is your fault! I shouldn't have made love to you that night. It was such a stupid thing to do. How could I ever expect that you'd be interested in me after what my father did?" He looked around, picked up another DVD, and threw it in the box.

God, what had she done? In a moment of weakness, she'd cursed both Mac and herself to be haunted by their actions. Why did she always do the wrong thing? Why couldn't she think before she acted?

"I am," she whispered. "Interested. And that night was my fault, don't blame yourself."

He pushed the box away and strode over to stand before her. She swallowed hard, but refused to be intimidated and step back.

"You did nothing wrong," he snapped. "Except wear those pajamas. The rest of it was all me."

"No," she said gently. "It wasn't. You don't think I'd been dreaming about you since I'd met you? You don't think I was standing there, silently begging you to kiss me?"

He stepped forward, and this time she had to retreat, except the wall was behind her, and there was nowhere to go. He leaned one hand on the wall beside her, looking down at her, and she couldn't tell whether he wanted to kiss her or yell at her. Possibly both.

His hot gaze rested on her lips, and his chest heaved. "You don't want this," he said through gritted teeth. "If we have sex again, you'll be furious with yourself, and then you'll hate me for it. And I don't want you to hate me, Fred."

"I won't hate you," she whispered. Was this what she wanted? They mustn't… they shouldn't… She thought about her father, and how angry he'd be right now that she was standing here, talking to the son of the man who'd betrayed him.

But it didn't matter. At that moment, what she felt for Mac overpowered everything else, as if he were the sun, blazing light that banished even the darkest shadows.

He looked into her eyes, and she knew he could see the truth.

"Fuck it," he said, his voice little more than a growl, and then he crushed his lips to hers.

SERENITY WOODS

Chapter Twenty-Two

Mac poured all the frustration he'd been feeling over the past week into the kiss. It had been the hardest week of his life. He'd watched Fred walking around, going about her day, talking to other people, eating, drinking, laughing, and his body had burned for her. The fact that she seemed to have cut herself off from him so easily had stung. Did she not feel anything for him? Was it all in his head?

In the end, he could cope with it no more, and he'd thrown his things in the ute, determined that night, at least, to have some peace, and hopefully he would cease to be plagued by thoughts of the woman who'd given herself to him so freely and so passionately.

And then she'd appeared in front of him, her long hair lifting in the evening breeze, and come into the house, and looked up at him with such longing in her eyes that he was lost.

His hands tightened on her arms, an involuntary gesture as he fought against his desire, but she didn't cry out. Instead, her mouth opened beneath his, and he swept his tongue inside. Passion flooded him as she moaned in approval, and he pushed her up against the wall.

Lifting his hands, he cupped her face, moving back so he could stare into her eyes, needing to reassure himself that she definitely wanted this. All he saw there was yearning and passion, so he kissed her again, gentler this time, his tongue playing with hers, enjoying the game, the slick slide that made his blood thunder through his body, made him so hard that his erection strained at his jeans.

Sometimes when you're hungry, nothing but fast food will suffice; however, at other times you want a culinary delight, and to savor each and every course. Last time had been quick, and now he wanted to draw out their pleasure, to make it last as long as he could.

The first thing he wanted to do was taste her.

He started by removing her T-shirt, drawing it up over her head and loving the way her hair lifted with it before flowing down over her shoulders like a bale of brown silk. She wore a lacy cream bra beneath it, and he spent a moment admiring the way the lace flowers adorned her breasts before sliding his hands behind her and releasing the clasp. He drew the straps down her arms and tossed the bra on the sofa, watching her breasts take their natural shape, her pale skin glowing in the light from the lamp. Fred sucked her bottom lip, obviously awkward about standing there half naked before him, but he didn't care. He traced across the swell of her left breast with a finger, then slipped his hand beneath to weigh it in his palm before brushing his thumb across her nipple. A sigh escaped her lips, and he bent to capture it, kissing her deeply as he teased her nipples to tight buttons with his fingers.

God, but he wanted this woman—he was at odds with himself, wanting to spend hours playing with her, teasing her, arousing her, and yet he ached, desperate to find his own pleasure in her soft body. He'd spent too many nights lying there in the darkness, fighting his passion as he'd played through his memories of that evening, remembering the way her wet skin had glistened, and how she'd filled the air with her sighs when she'd come.

"I want you," he said, his voice thick and hoarse as he slid his hands to her hips and splayed them there. He pushed her hard against the wall, and she gasped and sank her hands into his hair.

"Take me, then." She tugged his head and brought his lips to hers, and her kiss mirrored his desperation.

With a groan, he kissed along her jaw and down her neck, over her breast, and then closed his mouth over her nipple, savoring the sensation of her soft velvet skin against his tongue. He tugged it to a peak, then did the same with the other one, before dropping down onto his knees.

While teasing her belly button with his tongue, he undid her jeans, then slid them down her legs and held her so she could step out of them. She steadied herself by leaning on his shoulders, and he could hear her breathing, fast, irregular. Discarding her jeans, he focused on her panties, admiring the tiny scrap of cotton that barely covered her mound before pulling them down too.

Finally, she stood before him naked, just as he wanted it, just as he'd dreamed. He kissed over her belly, smoothing his hands down her silky thighs, then slid a hand beneath her left knee and lifted it, wrapping her leg around him. Leaning forward, he pressed his nose to her folds and inhaled, hearing her answering groan above him.

Jesus, there was nothing like the smell of a woman, deep and earthy, so fucking primeval that it reached into his DNA and awoke the caveman inside him.

He growled and slid his tongue into her, and Fred cried out and tightened her fingers in his hair. *Ahhh*, she was wet, and slick, and swollen, and she tasted divine, sweet and rich and creamy, better than the best Pinot Gris he'd ever had, and that was saying something.

His fingers parted, explored, delved inside her, while his tongue circled and teased, taking her closer to the edge with every fast flick and slow lick. He loved how abandoned she was, how she was standing here, in the living room, naked, wrapped around him, and she didn't care. She wasn't protesting that someone might see, and there wasn't a hint of reluctance about her. She matched him in all ways, and that was a treasure he hadn't expected, giving him an unfamiliar ache deep inside.

She was close, he could feel it, her muscles trembling, and she was holding her breath, her hips rocking to guide him as she felt her orgasm waiting in the wings. He slowed his pace, teased it out of her, and when she came he felt a flood of delight at her long gasps and cries of pleasure.

As if her legs would no longer keep her up, she slid down the wall. Mac caught her and fell backward, and she tumbled on top of him, all hair and soft skin and warm, wet mouth. He wrapped his arms around her, reveling in being enveloped by this woman. Her kiss was forceful, demanding, and she caught his hands in hers and pinned them above his head, straddling him and refusing to let him move.

"Mine," she said, looking into his eyes, just that one word, but it made his heart miss a beat and took his breath away, so all he could do was nod.

She leaned back and, without saying anything, she undid his belt and slid his zipper down, and then she was releasing his erection from his boxers and giving him long, slow strokes. Mac covered his face with his hands, feeling himself swell in her palm, and he groaned, conscious that she was teasing desire from him the same way he had her.

He wasn't going to last much longer. He was too keyed up, had wanted this for too long. He put a hand on her arm to stop her, and she took his hands and pinned them above him again, leaning over him. Her hair fell around him like a curtain, just the way he'd imagined it that first day he saw her.

Shifting up, she rocked her hips so the tip of his erection slid through her swollen, wet folds. He closed his eyes and groaned again.

Letting him part her, she paused at the point of penetration and kissed him. "I'm on the pill," she whispered. "But do you want to use a condom?"

He looked into her hazel eyes, swimming in their depths. Again, the caveman reared up inside him. He wanted to bury himself in her, wanted to spill inside her.

"No," he said.

Keeping her gaze fixed on his, she moved her hips, coating him with her moisture. Then, just as he was thinking this was the temptation of St. Mac and he was going to embarrass himself, she pushed down, and he slid inside her.

"*Aaahhh*," she said, exhaling with satisfaction, and he felt her relaxing her muscles, letting him in all the way.

It was divine, like a slipping into a warm bath on a cool day, and he closed his eyes and just *felt*, just enjoyed the sensation of joining with her, of being one.

"Mmm…" She took his hands and placed them on her breasts. Happy to help, he cupped them and played with her nipples while she rocked on top of him, arousing her again until her breathing grew deep and ragged, and he was sliding easily inside her, slick with her moisture.

She was moving, but it was too slow, and he loved slow and steady, but the caveman demanded he take her hard and fast. So he caught her around the waist, pushed up, and tipped her onto her back, doing his best to cushion her fall. The floor wasn't the most luxurious place for lovemaking, but he couldn't spare the time to take her to the bedroom—he wanted her here, now, and Fred seemed to feel the same, as she dug her nails in his back and wrapped her legs around his waist.

"Yes," she said, so he began to thrust, and soon lost himself in the blissful dance of it all, becoming little more than pleasure and sensation. The world faded away, and there was only Fred and her wet warmth and her hot mouth, and he wanted it to go on forever, to keep plunging into her, to hold onto the exquisite feeling that wasn't just physical, but emotional too, the overwhelming joy and beauty of having her in his arms, of being inside her, of joining with her in this most ancient of ways.

And then she was coming, clamping around him, so tight, so tight, and Mac gave in to the insistent demand of his muscles and let his climax claim him, spilling jet after jet into her warm, willing body. Sex was always good, but this was fucking sensational, and his orgasm seemed to go on forever, locking them in an eternal embrace, with her hands in his hair, her hazel eyes drinking in his bliss.

And then it released him, and he sagged on top of her, discovering he'd been holding his breath, which now came in giant gasps.

"Jesus." He tried not to flatten her, but it was difficult, as all the bones seemed to have disappeared from his body. "What do you do to me, woman?"

"Oh God. Mac." She groaned. "We're going to have to make it to the bedroom at some point. This floor feels like rock."

She was implying there would be a next time. He touched his nose to hers, then kissed her. "We will, I promise. I'm sorry."

"Don't apologize. It was... nice." She kissed him back.

Carefully, he withdrew from her and moved to one side, flopping onto his back. "Wow. Jeez."

"Mac? Can you... um... pass me a tissue?"

He glanced at her, then at the coffee table, extracted one from the box, and passed it to her.

"That's a first," he said, watching her.

She gave him a somewhat shy look. "Me too." She glanced over at where her clothes lay in a heap and laughed. The German Shepherd was lying on top of her clothes, her nose on her paws. "Poor Scully. I bet she wonders what we were doing."

"Eh, she's a dog of the world." He grinned. "Bed? For a cuddle?"

"Yeah, come on."

They went into the bedroom, and Mac stripped off while Fred climbed on. Then he slid in beside her. She turned onto her side to face him. He did the same, and they surveyed each other quietly while he ran a finger up her arm and over her shoulder, then played with her hair.

Mac watched thoughts and emotions passing behind her eyes like clouds on a summer day. She wasn't good at hiding her feelings, and he could see she felt embarrassed and shy and sexy at the memory of what they'd done, touched that he'd wanted her so badly he had to have her right there.

He saw the moment she remembered what had brought her to him, and why she was in New Zealand. The light dimmed from her eyes, and her smile faded away like morning mist.

"I wish he wasn't my father," he said.

She frowned. "You can't say that. He's half of what makes you what you are. I'm the same with my mother—I can't wish that because I wouldn't be here if it wasn't for her."

"Even so. I wish it had been someone else. With all my heart." He felt a twist inside, hard enough to make him wince. "Do you think you'll ever be able to look at me without thinking about my family and what we did to yours?"

"I…" She bit her lip. "I hope so. I am trying to forget."

But the doubt in her eyes told him the truth. He would always be James MacDonald's son, a symbol of the betrayal of her father and her mother's early grave.

To his surprise, she leaned close and touched her lips to his. "Tell me about him," she said.

"I don't want to talk about him, not now," he said, his voice a growl.

"I mean it. I only know what he did to my father, but there must have been more to him than that. What was he like before then? My father obviously thought him a good friend."

"They were." He twirled a strand of her hair around his finger. "They'd known each other since they were kids. Went to the same school. Learned about the vineyard together. From what I understand, Harry was always the explorer, the one who wanted to climb higher, go deeper into the bush, swim out farther from the shore. My father tagged along, but he was a home bird at heart. When Harry left New Zealand, his parents were already dead, so my father offered to take over the running of the estate, and Harry agreed."

He sighed. "Harry was gone for seven or eight years, as you know. He came back periodically, but the visits became more infrequent, and I suppose Dad gradually made more decisions about the estate by himself. By the time your father came back for good, Dad must have thought of the land as his own."

"But that was over twenty years ago," she said, puzzled. "They worked together for another... what? Fifteen years before my father died? Do you think your dad was secretly scheming all that time?"

"No, not actively. But I think he was stewing on it. He was already an alcoholic by then, and I think it was addling his brain."

"And what about his marriage? When did that go wrong?"

"I was very young, barely two years old, when they broke up. Mum doesn't like to talk about it, and he always acted as if she never existed. If he did talk about her, it was with real venom. He hated her, I think."

"Ouch. That must have been hard."

"Yeah."

She reached out a hand and trailed a finger through the hairs on his chest. "I wonder what went wrong between them? Was it his alcoholism?"

"Possibly."

"Although why would that make him hate her?"

"I don't know."

A frown marred her brow. "Do you think she might have had an affair?"

He lifted the strand of hair he was playing with to his nose. It smelled of mint, and made his mouth water. "I guess. What made you say that?"

"It's the only thing I can think of that would make him hate her."

He let the strand slide through his fingers. "It would make sense."

Then he froze. His gaze fixed on her, his eyes wide.

"What?" she said.

"What if..." He couldn't believe he was thinking it or about to say it, but the idea swept over him like a tidal wave. "What if she had an affair with someone, and got pregnant?"

Fred stared back. "You mean..."

"They'd been married for fifteen years before they had me. She told me they'd thought he was unable to have kids. And I'm an only child. What if I'm not actually James's son?"

Fred pushed herself up. "Seriously?"

He sat up too. "It would explain everything. Why he resented me his whole life. Why he was always so fucking horrible to me, both as a kid and as an adult. Why he turned to alcoholism, maybe even why he did that to your dad, because he was jealous of your dad talking about his three daughters."

Her jaw dropped. "Oh my God."

He sank his hands into his hair. "I can't believe I never thought of it before."

"You'll have to talk to your mother," she said. "Will it upset her?"

"I don't care if it will," he replied roughly. "I need to know the truth."

His head was spinning. He might not be James MacDonald's son. All this time he'd felt as if he had a seed of darkness inside him. For years, he'd worried the seed would take root and grow. And now…

"You wouldn't be Mac anymore," Fred said. "I'd have to call you something else."

"You could try my first name," he suggested.

She blinked at him.

"Eamon?" he reminded her. "Please tell me you didn't forget your husband's name."

"I forgot we were married," she said, and subsided into laughter.

He pulled her on top of him and covered her mouth with his until it stopped the giggles and she gave in and kissed him.

"Would it make our marriage illegal?" she whispered when he finally let her go. "If the name was wrong?"

"I don't know." He held his breath. "Is that what you want?"

He waited for her to say *it would make things easier*, or *only if it didn't invalidate the will*. But instead, she gave a tiny shake of her head.

He was married to this woman, in sickness and in health, until death parted them, and it was very possible that he wasn't James MacDonald's son. He hoped with all his heart that he wasn't. He wanted to be able to tell Fred that was the case, and watch her eyes fill with joy. It would wipe away all the pain and shadows of the past, and instead he could concentrate on having a real marriage, with a future. Maybe even with kids.

He saw his hope reflected in her eyes before she lowered her lips to his. *Please*, he whispered to the shadows in the room, to whoever might be listening, to God, if He was there.

Please.

Chapter Twenty-Three

Mac drove down the winding road toward Russell with a pounding heart.

Once he'd gotten the idea into his head about his mother having an affair, he hadn't been able to get rid of it. Even though he kept telling himself it was stupid, and that his mother would never have cheated, the more he thought about it, the more it made sense.

When he was younger, he could remember a man coming to visit his mother. His name had been David, and Mac vaguely remembered his mother and this David sitting in the kitchen talking while he played with his Lego on the floor, and taking walks around the garden while he kicked a football on the lawn. He didn't remember them being intimate at all, and he'd never given much thought to it, but now he began to wonder whether David had been more than a friend.

If that was the case, though, where was he now? Megan had dated a few guys over the years that he knew of, although not until he'd grown up and left home, and even then she'd been very discreet about it, so it was possible David was still on the scene, even though Mac wasn't aware of it. Had David remained in touched with her because they shared a link stronger than friendship?

If James wasn't his father, Mac wasn't sure why James hadn't refused to acknowledge him at all. He might have been a bad father, but he'd still called Mac his son.

It was a puzzle, and now he had the idea in his head, he needed to know the truth.

Fred had asked him to stay at the house, but that decision needed more discussion and thought. They'd made big steps forward tonight, but they weren't there yet, and neither of them were ready to move in together. He needed to get this sorted first, so he'd left her with a goodbye kiss and a promise to let her know what he'd found out, and headed down the hill to Russell.

SERENITY WOODS

The town was its usual lively self, the bars and restaurants spilling light out onto the pavements. The tables outside were half full, customers now wearing jackets or shawls to keep off the cool evening breeze. Autumn had truly arrived, he thought as he drove along the sea front toward his mother's house. Winter would be a few months yet, and even then, up here, it would be mild, but he could smell it in the air.

He reached the end of The Strand and turned into Wellington Street, drove a little way, then pulled up outside his mother's home. This wasn't where he had grown up—that had been right in the middle of town. Megan MacDonald had moved here after her divorce, when a bitter James had all but forced her out of the family home. Another move that puzzled Mac. If a marriage failed, even if there had been arguments and sadness, it took some doing for a man to make life so unpleasant for his wife and two-year-old that she felt the need to move out.

Leaving his stuff in the ute for now, he let Scully out of the back, and they walked up the garden path, past the hostas and begonias growing in pots, to the front door, and rang the bell.

"I'll have to get you a key," Megan said as she opened the door. "Can't have you waking me up at all hours of the night. Hey, Scully-dog." She ruffled the dog's ears.

"Yeah, because I'll be out at all the nightclubs until the early hours." Mac gave her a wry look as he passed her.

"You're a babe-in-arms," she said, following him into the living room. "You should be out partying the night away."

"Mum, I'm thirty-two. And anyway, I'm married."

"Ha! How is Fred, by the way?" She walked over to the cabinet where she kept her alcohol, took out a bottle of Islay malt, and showed it to him.

"No, thanks." He wanted a clear head for the conversation.

Raising her eyebrows, she replaced the bottle. "Tea, then?"

"Sure."

She went into the tiny kitchen and started sorting out the mugs. "You didn't answer me—how is Fred?"

Fantastic. Sexy. Beautiful. "She's good." He scratched behind Scully's ears, thinking about how he'd taken Fred on the floor. He definitely had to get her to the bed next time, and he had to slow things down. Fast and furious was fun, but she deserved better than that.

Megan cast him a glance before putting the teabags in. "Anything you want to tell me?"

His heart began to race again. "About what?"

"About you and Fred?"

He blew out a breath. "No. But I do want to talk to you about something."

"Oh?" She took out the teabags and poured in some milk, stirred the mugs, then brought them into the living room. "That sounds ominous."

"It kind of is. It's serious."

"Oh dear." She sipped her tea. "Is Fred pregnant?"

His eyes widened. "No! Jesus. Nothing like that."

She just smiled at him over the rim of the mug.

He tried to thrust away the idea of Fred at his side, pregnant and barefoot, and concentrated on his mother. "No, this is about you—about us."

Her smile faded and she sat back. "Okay."

"Mum, there's something I have to ask you." He paused, suddenly embarrassed. He respected his mother, who had brought him up almost single-handed, and who had remained his most loyal advocate through his life.

"What is it?" she prompted.

"I don't want to insult you," he said softly.

She tipped her head to the side. "Come on, sweetheart. Nothing you could say would insult me. You're my boy—you always will be. Is this about your father?"

"Kind of. Mum… I need to know… before I was born… did you have an affair?"

Her eyes widened so fast it was almost comical. "What?"

"Only I've been thinking," he said, the words tumbling out fast now he'd said it, "how I don't really look like Dad, and we're not similar in character at all. And how it took him so long to get you pregnant. And I wondered if he's not my father, and that's why he's resented me all these years. I'm sorry to ask, but I was thinking about it, and I had to know…"

She held up a hand. "Sweetheart, it's okay. I'm not offended. I understand why you wanted to know. I'm not sure why you're asking now. I expected this years ago." She looked into his eyes, and he saw realization dawn. "Ah," she whispered. "Fred."

He swallowed hard. Leaning forward, elbows on his knees, he waited for her to answer.

She looked at her mug for a long time. Then, finally, she said, "I'm sorry to tell you this…"

He held his breath.

"…But no, I never had an affair. James MacDonald is your father. There's no doubt about it."

He stared at her. He couldn't believe it. It had made perfect sense, and now it all came crashing down around his ears.

"You're sure?" he asked.

Her lips curved up. "Am I sure that I didn't have an affair? Yes, Mac, I'm sure."

He closed his eyes. What a stupid question. But he couldn't believe it. "Then… why did the two of you break up when I was so young?"

"Because of his drinking. He was such a jealous man, and he was jealous of the attention you demanded of me when you were a baby. He drank too much even then, and one night he got drunk when he was supposed to be looking after you, when I had a rare night out with a friend. He left you crying in the cot for hours. I was so angry, I walked out with you that night. We hardly said two words to each other after that."

"Why have you never told me any of this?"

"Because you never asked, and Mac, I've always tried hard not to put your father down in your hearing. He was far from perfect, but he was your father, and I never wanted to come between the two of you."

She moved to sit on the sofa beside him. "I can see how it would have been the answer to some of your problems if James hadn't been your father. But it is what it is."

"I hate it." Leaning forward, he sank his hands into his hair. "I hate having his blood in my veins. It's like poison—I can feel it coursing around me, tainting everything it touches."

"Mac." Her voice was sterner this time. "You have to learn to deal with this. You can't spend the rest of your life hating him."

"Can't I?" He threw a glare at her. "I've had him hanging around my neck like a millstone all my life. He spent years putting me down, telling me I was worthless, that I'd never amount to anything. Why? If he really was my father, why did he do that?"

He'd thought she would get angry, but instead she just smiled. "Because you were better than he was. Can't you see that? He was jealous of you, Mac. You were more intelligent, warmer, wittier, better looking... You worked hard. You weren't lazy. You were determined to make something of yourself. He fell into working at Blue Penguin Bay because Harry persuaded him to. James wasn't into the vineyard. He didn't give a damn about the estate. He saw a chance of an easy job, and he took it."

Mac stared at her. "I didn't know that."

"Of course, over the years he picked up some knowledge about it just by watching Harry and the other guys around him, but how do you think he felt when you went to university and got a degree, then spent years learning your trade at different vineyards across the world? He hated it when you came back with new ideas. It made him feel stupid and out-of-date. And he wasn't the sort of man to say 'hey son, show me what you know.' He was far too old school for that."

"I never thought about it," Mac whispered. He'd just wanted to show his old man how they could make the place better.

She sighed. "Something you should know is that Harry told him near the end that he considered you the son he'd never had. Harry loved you, and you shared a bond that James envied—both in the sense of a relationship, and in the sense of loving Blue Penguin Bay. I think that may have been behind what James did at the end."

"I never knew that." He felt a surge of fondness for Harry, who had always treated him with kindness and respect. In another world, they might have been closer, and maybe Harry might have named Mac as his heir, but the man had possessed his own demons, and his family in the U.K. had obviously never been far from his thoughts.

Megan squeezed her son's fingers, bringing his attention back to her. "James was weak, and petty, and he could be spiteful, but he did have some good attributes. He was faithful to me while we were married. And I loved him for many years. When a woman is young, she often finds a particular type of male confidence sexy, until she realizes it's not just confidence, it's arrogance. But he was fun and flirty when we were young. He wasn't all bad. And you must remember that just because you're his son, it doesn't mean you have to be like him. His weaknesses don't run in your veins, Mac, only his blood."

Mac stood and went over to the window. He looked out at the Pacific Ocean, which churned, thick and dark like treacle, under the cloudy sky.

His emotions were churning in the same way, stirring up lots of feelings he'd hoped to keep buried. What his mother had said made sense, and cleared up some of his frustration behind not knowing why his father had seemed to dislike him so much. It didn't make it any easier to bear, but at least he felt as if he understood it now.

But it hadn't solved his main problem. He was still James MacDonald's son. The son of the man who had betrayed Harry Cartwright. Who had tried to take away Fred, Sandi, and Ginger's inheritance.

What if his mother was wrong? If James's character did run in his veins? All his life, Mac had striven to ensure he wasn't like his father, but there had to be some similarities, didn't there? He didn't feel as if he had alcoholic tendencies—he liked a drink the same as the next man, but he didn't have that urge to keep drinking, to keep filling up his glass. But what if deeper, nastier things lurked beneath his skin, like the Loch Ness Monster under the lake? How did he know they wouldn't surface in the years to come?

Ultimately, it didn't matter what he thought. The fact was that Fred had difficulty looking at him without thinking of what his father had done to Harry, and he wasn't sure that would ever go away. She was attracted to him, and the attraction felt fierce and strong, but he didn't know if it was powerful enough to overcome the deep sense of betrayal she felt toward his family.

"She'll come around," his mother said behind him. "She won't want to lose you."

But Mac wasn't so sure.

Chapter Twenty-Four

The next day dawned bright, but clouds were gathering on the horizon, promising rain.

Eleven o'clock found Fred sitting on the garden seat at the front of the house, overlooking the vineyard with the Pacific Ocean in the background, when her sister walked up to her.

"I've been looking for you," Sandi said, sitting beside her. "I found a nice aerial photograph of the vineyard in the back cupboard, and I wasn't sure if you'd want it for the house."

"Oh lovely, thanks. I'll take a look at it in a little while."

Sandi nodded. Then she gave her sister a shrewd look. "You okay?"

Fred looked down at the phone in her hand, then slid it into her pocket. "Not really."

"What's the matter?"

Fred let out a long breath. "Mac and I were talking last night about why his parents broke up, and we started thinking that maybe his mother had had an affair. She'd been married to James for fifteen years before Mac was born, and it just seemed odd that she'd suddenly get pregnant, and then they'd get divorced. Mac started to think that maybe he wasn't James's son."

"Oh my God."

"He was so excited. We both were. I didn't realize until that moment how much I hated that James was his father, and what a shadow it cast over us."

"And? What happened?"

"He spoke to his mum last night. She said she'd never had an affair. He's definitely James's son."

Sandi surveyed her for a long moment. Then she sat back, looking out at the view.

"I wanted someone else to be his father so badly," Fred whispered.

"What difference would it have made?" Sandi asked.

Fred frowned at her. "You really have to ask that?"

"I do. How would it have changed how you feel about him? What difference would it have made to your relationship?"

"It would have made all the difference!" Fred couldn't believe her sister didn't understand. "I like him, Sandi. And he likes me. Against all the odds, I think we could have had something going. But what James did… It hangs over us all the time. I can't get rid of it. It's always in the back of my mind."

Sandi turned on the bench to face her. She had a curious look on her face. "And you're saying that you won't consider a relationship with him because it didn't turn out that he had a different father?"

"How can I?" Hot tears filled Fred's eyes, but she refused to let them fall. How could she explain to Sandi the burning disappointment at the news that he was, after all, James's son? When he'd gone, she'd hardly been able to sleep, so excited at the thought that they might be free. And then she'd got his call, and it had all come crashing down.

"I hate James," she said, breathing heavily. "I can't bear to think of Dad entrusting everything to him, only for James to stab him in the back. He was here, alone, thinking his daughters didn't want anything to do with him, and yet he still left us his vineyard. He still loved us. He would have been so upset if he'd found out what James had done."

Sandi nodded slowly. "That's true. I'm not saying that what James did wasn't a terrible betrayal. But sweetie, we know that Mac violently disagrees with what his father did. It would have been far easier for him to say nothing, to keep the estate for himself, and never admit what had happened. But he didn't. Even though he was convinced we'd be furious with him, he told the truth and prepared to face the music. That was an incredibly courageous thing to do, don't you think?"

"Yes, but—"

"We could have taken him to court, demanded some kind of retribution for any profits we'd lost."

"I know, but—"

"You're punishing him for what his father did," Sandi said. "Do you really think that's fair?"

Fred opened her mouth, then shut it again. She thought for a moment. Then she said, "That's not what it's about. I'm not punishing him."

"No? You don't think he's partly responsible for what James did?"

"In what way?"

"I don't know, in any way? Do you think that he should have paid more attention to what was going on at the estate, forced James to show him the books?"

"No. I don't blame him for that."

"Then…"

"It's like James is a ghost hovering over him," Fred said softly. "In just the same way that I feel Dad's watching over us."

"Do you?" Sandi's eyebrows rose.

"All the time. And I can't help but think that he's furious with me."

Now Sandi was looking pained. "Why?"

"Because I should have pushed more to get in contact with him. And… I should have known when he died."

"How should you have known?"

"I should have felt it. In my heart. I can't believe that he'd been dead for so long when we found out." A tear finally spilled down Fred's cheek. "That's just awful. He had none of his family here—he only had James, and that makes me feel as if someone's pushing a sword into my heart." Her voice shook.

"Hey, it's all right." Sandi put an arm around her and hugged her. "Why have you never told me before that you feel like this?"

"I don't know, we just never got around to it. We all focused on how angry we were, and of course there was Mum…" Fred leaned forward and put her face in her hands.

"Sweetie…" Sandi wrapped her other arm around her and hugged her tightly. "You have to let go of this guilt and blame, otherwise it eats away at you, and I'm talking from experience here. We've all had such an awful time over the past few years—it's not surprising that we're desperate to find someone to blame for all the hurt we've suffered. But look, life happens. Some of it's good, and some of it's bad. People aren't perfect. Some of them are mean, and nearly all are selfish. But few people are truly evil. Did James do wrong by changing the will? Of course he did. Was he evil? I don't believe that. I doubt he sat there planning it for years. He and Dad were friends—

I can't imagine that Dad would have worked with him for so long if he thought James resented him deep down. I think James saw an opportunity and took it. Who knows why? Jealousy, envy, greed… These are age-old emotions, and none of us are free of them."

Fred wiped her face, then looked out at the Pacific, which was the color of Mac's eyes. "I know you're right…"

"Maybe James was desperate to hurt us," Sandi continued, "but I doubt it. I doubt he even gave us a second thought. He was only thinking of himself. And we don't know what he would say if he were here now. He might say that he hated Dad and his family and we got everything we deserved. But we don't know that. He might see what his actions have done, and he might say sorry."

Fred doubted it, but she appreciated her sister trying to help.

"The point I'm making—somewhat badly," Sandi said, "is that it seems pointless to me to pour all your energy into hating James. And even more pointless is to resent Mac for being his son. From what I've seen, Mac would never do anything like what his father did. And you have to ask yourself, do you truly believe the sins of the father should pass to the child? When Mum died owing all that money on her credit cards and there wasn't enough left in her estate to pay them, the debt was wiped. That was because the rule is the child isn't responsible for what the parent does in his or her life."

Fred rubbed her nose. "That's true."

Sandi kissed her forehead. "Mum shouldn't have burned Dad's letters, and James shouldn't have changed the will. Things would have been very different if either of those things hadn't happened. But they did, and it's too late to change them now. We can only deal with the consequences."

"I wish I could be like you," Fred whispered. "I wish I could just put everything behind me. But I feel as if I'm caught up in a loop. I keep thinking about those moments when I could have changed everything. If only I'd tried to phone Dad, if only I hadn't yelled at Mum and walked out… if only…"

"That's natural, and it's a part of grief. But we've been given this incredible opportunity." Sandi gestured at the vines in front of them, now mostly free of grapes, ready to start the process all over again. "We have the vineyard, and the restaurant, and the B&B. We've escaped the place that holds so many memories for us, and we can start all over again. And you…" She squeezed Fred's shoulders.

"You've met Mac. Who'd have thought the two of you would fall in love?"

"Love?" Fred stared at her.

"You love him, Fred. Of course you do! And he loves you. It's written all over his face."

Fred's jaw dropped. "But..."

"What more could you want? He's gorgeous, he's incredibly honest, and you're already married to him!" Sandi laughed. "You think Ginger and I didn't pray that the two of you would get together? We saw a spark between you the day we arrived here. Not everyone has the opportunity to find love, and you simply can't let it go without giving it a chance."

Fred didn't know what to say. Her heart raced as she looked at her sister's pleading face. Poor Sandi, who thought she'd found the man of her dreams only to discover that he'd hidden a terrible secret from her for years. Was she right? Should Fred put aside her blame and resentment and be honest about her feelings for Mac?

What was the alternative? Was she really prepared to say to him that she would never be able to see past his father?

"I'll leave you to think about it," Sandi said, rising. "But don't take too long. Opportunities are like balloons, and we have to grab them while we can or sometimes they just float away." Giving her sister a parting smile, Sandi walked back to the B&B.

Fred watched her go, then turned her gaze back to the view. Mac had said something similar: *You're like a balloon seller in a city, who occasionally lets go of a balloon and watches it rise into the sky until he can't see it anymore.* How strange that they'd used a similar analogy.

The clouds hadn't moved from the horizon, and the sky above her was a clear blue, the Pacific a slightly darker shade beneath it. The color of Mac's eyes. She shivered as she thought of them staring into hers the night before while he moved inside her. She hadn't planned for that to happen—she just hadn't wanted him to go. But when she'd seen him, the longing had turned into a deep desire she hadn't been able to hold back.

She sighed. Her father would have sat on this seat just a few years ago, looking out at the same view. It gave her a strange feeling in her tummy to think that.

Among the vines, the shadows formed the figure of a man. Fred's heart rate increased, but she sat still, her gaze fixed on it. It wasn't a man, it was just shadows. But her skin prickled all the same.

"Are you there?" she asked her father.

Silence remained, but she imagined she heard a whisper on the breeze. *Yes…*

"I'm sorry," she said. "I wish I'd contacted you. I wish I could have gotten to know you, and visited you. And I wish I'd been there when you died."

She heard no words, and yet around her, the air changed—the temperature dropped, and she felt the touch of fingers on her cheek. Or was it just the wind?

"Mac's right," she said. "You made your will the way you did because you thought that would be best for me, and for Sandi and Ginger. I'm sure you hoped it would encourage us to settle down. You could never have foreseen what James would do. I know you thought he was your friend. I hope that, wherever you are, you can forgive him for what he did. I'm not sure I can, but I will try. What's done is done."

She took a deep breath. "And I hope you've made your peace with Mum, and she with you. I hope neither of you blame me for the things I've done. I would never have hurt either of you intentionally. I love you both from the bottom of my heart."

It was tough, growing up, she thought. Making decisions for yourself, ones that you weren't always sure your parents would approve of. Moving on, to a new life that didn't involve them. And letting go, when they'd gone.

Beside her, on the seat, was a single dry red leaf, a symbol of the season. She picked it up and held it by the stem for a moment, feeling the autumn wind tugging at it, wanting to play. Then she opened her fingers and released it. It fluttered up into the air, spun around a few times, and then it was gone, spirited away by the breeze to join its brothers and sisters in the vineyard.

She watched it go, and smiled.

Chapter Twenty-Five

The harvest was nearly over. In the bright sunshine, Mac was walking along the vines, Scully at his heels, running his fingers over the leaves while the dog snuffled along the ground.

Stopping for a moment, he raised an arm to check his watch. The day before, he'd sent Fred a text asking her to meet him at the vineyard at two o'clock on Sunday. The digits read 1:50. Ten minutes to go. Lowering his arm again, he stuffed his hands in his pockets and walked on.

He hoped he'd made the right decision. He could be about to make the biggest mistake of his life. Then again, not doing what he was about to do would be an even bigger mistake. Better to regret the things you did rather than the things you hadn't done, he kept telling himself. Hopefully, that little epithet would still ring true after two o'clock.

Fred had replied to his text with *No worries* and a smiley face. He hoped that was a good sign.

He hadn't spoken to her since he'd called to tell her that James was definitely his father. She'd listened to the news quietly, and hadn't reacted at all, finishing by telling him that she'd see him on Monday.

He'd spent that night walking along the beach, miserable and unhappy. His first thought was that he should tell her he was going to leave Blue Penguin Bay and get a job in another vineyard. Maybe down in the South Island, he thought, right down, in Otago. As far away from her as he could get.

He couldn't continue to work alongside her without being able to touch her. He just couldn't. His body hungered for her. He thought about her all the time, and he dreamed about her at night. She had an inner beauty that would haunt him for the rest of his days. He suspected she would have had a capacity to love him as deep as the ocean, and that would have been something truly sensational, except for the fact that the events of their past held it in check.

How could he survive if he stayed? It would be torture, and Mac was tired of torturing himself. It was time he put his ghosts to rest, accepted who he was, and moved on. He needed to find himself another *turangawaewae*. Some other place to stand.

The thought had physically hurt.

So he'd continued walking. It had been a windy night, and the dark waves had lashed at the shore, seemingly echoing the churning emotions inside him.

He couldn't leave. Neither the bay, nor Fred. He loved them both too much.

And gradually, like a pearl forming in the depths of an oyster, he'd started to formulate another plan.

A movement at the house caught his eye, and he stopped. It was Fred, leaning against the wall of the B&B, watching him. When she saw that she'd been spotted, she started walking toward him.

Tucking his hands in the pockets of his jeans, he watched her approach.

She walked slowly, her long green skirt blowing about her legs. She wore a russet-colored top and her chestnut hair hung in a braid over her shoulder. She looked like Autumn herself, bringing change, bringing an end to summer.

Jesus, he loved this woman. Was that possible in so short a time? He didn't know, and he didn't care. What did it matter if it was possible or right? His feelings were far too strong to be anything but love.

Harry, he begged her father, *if you're watching, give us your blessing. Make this go well.*

Fred approached and stopped a few feet in front of him. Her hazel eyes studied him, wisps of hair blowing across her forehead.

"Hey," she said.

"Hey." His throat felt scratchy, his voice little more than a squeak. He cleared his throat and tried again. "How are you?"

"I'm good. How have you been?"

"Fine, thanks." Polite as strangers.

Heart pounding, he glanced out to sea. Boats were sailing toward the horizon, heading out to bring in the day's catch. The sun was so bright it hurt his eyes.

He looked back at Fred. Her cheeks were a little flushed, and her lips curved up a tiny bit at the corners. Did she have any idea why he'd asked to meet her today?

"I have something for you," he said softly.

Her eyes widened, and her smile faded. "Oh," she whispered. "Is it... a going away gift?"

So she'd guessed what had been going through his mind, that he felt he couldn't stay if they weren't together. She looked truly miserable. His heart leapt. Not at her misery, but at what it implied.

"No." He withdrew his hand from his pocket, and showed her the velvet box, about four inches square. Without saying anything else, he opened it and showed her the contents.

Two gold wedding rings sat on the black velvet, side by side, one slightly bigger than the other. They glinted in the autumn sunlight.

"Marry me," he said.

Her jaw dropped. "Huh?"

He blew out a breath. He was going to have to do this the hard way.

Dropping to one knee, he took her hand. "Marry me again, Winifred Cartwright. Properly, this time. With rings, and vows, and a white wedding dress. Marry me, and make me the happiest man on earth."

He stared up at her. He felt a little queasy as she continued to stare at him as if he'd asked her to move to Venus. *Harry*, he begged in his mind. *Please...*

"Oh my God," she said. "Mac, get up."

His throat tightened, and he rose awkwardly to his feet. He'd fucked up. He'd left it too long. She didn't want him to stay, and...

"Oh my God," she said again, and to his surprise and utter shock, she threw her arms around his neck. "Oh Mac."

He inhaled deeply, stunned at the feel of her soft body against his, at the press of her lips repeatedly against his mouth. "Is that a yes?"

*

"Yes, yes, yes!" Fred laughed and kissed him again. She felt so happy it was like Christmas Day and her birthday all rolled into one. "I can't believe it—I thought you were about to tell me you were leaving." Her eyes filled with tears. "I was about to beg you not to go."

"Really?" He tightened his arms around her until she thought her bones might snap, but she didn't complain. She rested her forehead on his shoulder, and felt him press his lips to her hair. "I did think about it," he murmured. "I knew I couldn't stay here and be with you all day every day unless we were together. But I don't want to leave. I love Blue Penguin Bay, and I love you, Winifred Cartwright, with all my heart. I've never felt this way about another woman."

"And I've never felt like this about a man."

He moved back a little, cupped her face with his large hands, and looked into her eyes. "I meant it, about getting married properly. What we did was soulless, and I want to do it properly. I want to write my own vows, and promise to love you forever. To love and to cherish, until death do us part."

Tears rolled down her cheeks. "Me, too. I love you, Mac. I think I fell in love with you the moment I got out of the car and saw you standing there."

He brushed her tears away with his thumbs. "And the fact that I'm James's son... It's not a problem?"

She shook her head. "I had a long talk with Sandi, and she made me see that I need to put aside my blame and guilt. What's the point in holding on to it? It's like acid or poison—all it does is eat away at you. I've been so caught in the past that it's been impossible for me to look forward. Well, I'm not going to look back anymore. I'm going to keep my eyes front all the time, and concentrate on the future, not on the things I can't do anything about."

"There's nothing wrong with remembering the past," he said. "Or with feeling sad because of the way things turned out, or that we've lost those we love. But you're right that we have to think about ourselves. The way we feel about each other—it would be a crime if we didn't make the most of this."

Her heart swelled. "You really want to stay with me? Here, at the bay?"

"Right here. We have all the time in the world to work together on the vineyard and make it award-winning again. You wait, Fred, it's going to be fantastic here. With the restaurant and the B&B, and all the enthusiasm and energy that you girls have brought, they'll be talking about Blue Penguin Bay from Cape Reinga to Dunedin."

She slid her arms around his waist, and he wrapped his around her. It was a cool day, the breeze a trifle cold, but within his arms she felt protected from the worst of it, safe against the world.

"I hope my father is happy, wherever he is," she said.

"I asked for his blessing," Mac replied, surprising her. "I'm sure that if he hadn't approved of us getting together, he would have stopped us somehow. Anyway, why wouldn't he approve, Fred? He knows how we feel about each other. This is exactly what he wanted—you happily married, living at the bay, working on his vineyard."

"I suppose. I wish he was here with us so I could say thank you, and tell him I love him."

"He's here, sweetheart. I'm convinced of it. And your mother too. Our loved ones don't leave us."

He'd told her something similar on one of their early walks around the vineyard. *Harry's still here, somewhere, watching you now.* Before she met Mac, she'd thought of a person's soul as being tied to wherever their body was buried or their ashes scattered. Leaving the U.K. had been difficult when she'd thought that she'd left her mother behind. But Mac made her feel as if her parents were with her, at rest, content and happy now without the pressures of life that weighed a person down so badly.

She raised onto her toes and pressed her lips to his. "I love you," she said.

He slid his hands onto her butt, tightened his fingers on the muscles there, and lifted her a little, molding her to him while he kissed her properly with his tongue and lips and a graze of his teeth, until she sighed and melted in his arms.

"I think we should retire to the house," he murmured, moving his hips to illustrate his train of thought, in case she hadn't already guessed.

"It's the middle of the day," she said with a laugh, heart soaring.

"Sun's over the yardarm somewhere in the world. Come on. I fancy some afternoon delight."

Fred squealed as he bent and picked her up in his arms, then kissed him as he began to walk up to the house. "You won't be able to carry me all the way."

"Maybe not," he said with a groan, and lowered her down again. He grabbed her hand. "I'll drag you instead." And he pulled her along as he began to jog.

Laughing, Fred ran alongside him, following the line of vines back up to the house, Scully dancing at their feet.

At one point, she thought she saw the shadow of a man in the leaves, watching them. But this time, it didn't scare her, and she just smiled.

Blue Penguin Bay

Book 1: As Deep as the Ocean

Book 2: As Beautiful as the Bay

Book 3: As Timeless as the Sea

*

Excerpt from As Beautiful as the Bay (Book 2)

"Do you know the muffin man?" asked Ellie, the new young waitress.

Ginger wiped down the last stainless-steel counter and took the cloth over to the sink. "The muffin man? Who lives down Drury Lane?"

"Ha ha." Ellie stuck her tongue out and clipped the dishwasher shut. "You know who I mean. The sexy baker."

Ginger gave her an amused look as she rinsed the cloth. "You mean Sam Pankhurst?"

"He's the sexy one, right?"

"Oh, I don't know if I'd go that far. He's all right, I guess, if you like scruffy and grumpy and grouchy. And other dwarves."

Ellie looked puzzled. "Are we talking about the same guy? Runs the *All or Muffin* bakery?"

"Yeah. Are you going to make a joke about his buns now?"

"Quite possibly," Ellie said, unfazed. "He has a great bum."

"Ellie!"

The young woman laughed. "Well he has! Really nice and..." She held up her hands, fingers curved, and made a movement as if she were squeezing something firm and squidgy.

"Jesus." Ginger put the cloth into the washing box and cast a last glance around the room. "Okay, I think we're done for the day."

It was five p.m. on Sunday, and Ginger could have slept for a fortnight. Three months of working ten-hour days, seven days a week, was starting to take its toll. Air New Zealand would have made her pay an extra luggage allowance for the bags under her eyes.

"I go in the bakery every morning for a muffin," Ellie grumbled, "but he's always out the back, working. So… I was thinking… maybe you'd put in a good word for me?" She turned hopeful eyes to Ginger.

"Ellie." Phil, the sous chef, collected up the tea towels and threw them into the washing basket on top of Ginger's cloth. "For God's sake. Sam Pankhurst's one of the finalists for the Bay of Islands Gold Food Awards. I hardly think Ginger's going to be in the mood to be playing matchmaker."

Ellie's mouth formed an O. "Shit! I didn't realize. Sorry."

"It's all right." Ginger picked up the basket. "I'll take this through to the laundry room, and then I'm heading off. Can you lock up, Phil?"

He nodded, and she flashed them a smile, then headed off down the corridor.

In the laundry room, relieved to be alone at last, she blew out a long breath, then loaded the washing machine. Once it was going, she left via the back door, walked around the edge of the building, and sat on the wooden bench that overlooked the vineyard.

For a while she just sat there, too tired to move.

She felt frazzled, and not only from the long hours. Ellie's words had nipped at her nerve endings like a school of piranha. It wasn't the waitress's fault—she'd only been working at Blue Penguin Bay's restaurant for a few weeks. She wasn't to know about the riptide that flowed beneath the apparently calm waters.

Ginger looked out across the fields of vines that sloped down to the sparkling Pacific Ocean, and shivered. It was nearly shortest day, June twenty-first, and she missed the warm evenings she'd experienced when she'd first arrived in New Zealand. The websites hadn't lied when they'd described the Northland as the 'winterless north', and the temperature hadn't dropped anywhere near freezing yet, but the days had cooled, and Ginger was a summer girl at heart.

"Hey. Are you actually sitting down? I need to call the Guinness Book of Records."

Ginger looked over her shoulder to see her sister, Winifred, approaching with a smile. "Hey." She patted the bench next to her. "How's your day been?"

"Long." Fred sat beside her and yawned. "I'm worn out."

Ginger grinned. "Mac keeping you up late, is he?"

"Worn out from working," Fred corrected wryly. Then her lips twisted. "But yeah. I'm not getting a lot of sleep." Her arranged marriage to the vineyard's estate manager had eventually morphed into a real one, and the two of them had been living together for three months. Fred looked so happy at the thought of being chained to the marital bed that it brought a lump to Ginger's throat.

"How are you?" Fred asked.

"Good. The new spicy fish bites were a real hit. We're definitely keeping those on the menu."

"That's great." Fred put her arm around her and gave her a hug. "You okay?"

Ginger gave her a puzzled look. "Yeah, why?"

"Phil asked me to check on you."

Ginger rolled her eyes. "I'm fine."

"Come on Ging, spit it out. Phil wouldn't have said that if he wasn't worried about you. Something bothering you?"

Ginger lifted her face to the last rays of the setting sun and briefly closed her eyes. She didn't want to discuss it, but Fred wouldn't give up if she thought one of her sisters had a problem they needed to discuss. "Ellie made a comment about Sam, that's all."

"Ah."

Ginger narrowed her eyes. "Don't start."

"I said 'ah'. How's that starting something?"

"It was the way you said it."

Fred pursed her lips. "Has he asked you out this week?"

"Yeah. On Wednesday."

"And you said no?"

"Of course I said no."

Fred tipped her head to the side. "He's pretty persistent. Have you thought that maybe the way you're feeling is because deep down, you'd like to date him?"

"No! Absolutely not! A hundred and ten percent no. Not even if there'd been a zombie invasion, and he was the last man on Earth and we had to repopulate the planet."

"Right." Fred chewed her bottom lip. "You don't think that would be even a tiny bit fun?"

Irritation swept over her. "What do you want me to say? If you're hoping I'm going to admit I'm secretly in love with him, you're going to be in for a long wait."

"Who said anything about love? You can't deny that there's a zing between the two of you. I'm just surprised you haven't had a fling."

Ginger couldn't deny it. When she'd first set eyes on Sam Pankhurst, at Mac and Fred's wedding at the vineyard, she'd felt the thud of Cupid's arrow deep inside. Not in her heart—the tingle of attraction had been farther south than that. But it was there, and she knew Sam felt the same, because he'd asked her out on a date once a week since then, every week, without fail.

"Is this about the award?" Fred asked gently.

"Of course it's about the award." The familiar stab of hurt made her stomach clench.

Fred eyed her evenly. "I think you're viewing it all wrong."

"What other way can I view it? He didn't enter for the award, Fred, not until he discovered that I'd entered for it. And now he's determined to beat me to the finish line." She gritted her teeth with indignation. "You've seen what little he's done to promote the bakery. But it's a family business. The locals bought their bread there when his dad owned it, and probably before then. He's going to win all the local votes with zero effort." The thought of seeing the Gold Food Awards badge on *All or Muffin's* sign outside the bakery made her feel sick with fury.

"You stand every chance," Fred soothed. "Come on, all the local papers are full of Blue Penguin Bay. Everyone's talking about the vineyard and the way you've overhauled the restaurant. People are coming from all over the Northland, and farther afield, to eat here. We're having to turn people away."

"That doesn't mean I'll win."

"No..." Fred frowned. "I don't understand why this is so important. We knew it would take time to make the vineyard work, as well as its restaurant and bed and breakfast. We've actually done much better than we thought we would when we first came here.

Don't you remember the despair we all felt when Mac told us what his father had done?"

"Yes, of course." The memory was not a pleasant one. Ginger, Fred, and their other sister, Sandi, had come to New Zealand to take over the running of the Blue Penguin Bay estate following the death of their father, only to discover that James MacDonald, the previous estate manager, had spent all the profits and run the estate into the ground. The girls' father, Harry Cartwright, had, for some bizarre reason they still didn't completely understand, tied up their inheritance for when they got married. Desperate to right the wrongs of his father, Mac had proposed to Fred after only a week so she could access her share of the money. Luckily, the two of them had fallen in love, so the story had a happy ending, and Fred's fifty thousand dollars had gone a long way to restoring some of the estate's former glory.

"I'm thrilled with what we've achieved," Ginger said. "You and Mac have worked so hard on the vineyard, and Sandi's done wonders with the B&B. But the restaurant..." She hesitated.

"Is yours," Fred finished with a smile.

Ginger sighed, a little ashamed. "Yeah."

"And getting the Gold Food Award would make you feel as if you made the right decision coming here."

"Yes." Ginger knew her sister understood. Emigrating to the other side of the world from England had been tough on all of them. It didn't matter that they'd been glad to see the back of the U.K. after their mother died, nor that they all loved their new home.

Adjusting to a new culture—even one that seemed so similar to England's at first glance—had been harder than any of them had expected. They'd come to 'Godzone' on a work permit, but had all applied for permanent residency after Fred and Mac had decided to make their marriage a real one. Soon, they would have all the same rights as those born in the country.

But Ginger didn't feel like a Kiwi. She had an English accent, and English ways, and always would have. People frequently asked her if she was there on holiday, and she suspected that would probably happen even when she'd been living there for twenty years. Winning this award would be the first step to feeling as if the country was accepting her. For a start, award winners went forward into a national competition, which would be a huge thing for her considering she'd only recently started up.

But it wasn't just that. Back in England, she'd been terribly betrayed by the man she'd loved, or thought she'd loved, and it had ruined her career, as well as her love life. The award had become a symbol of her new start. It would be a confirmation that everything was going to be all right. That she was going to be able to pull herself up by her bootstraps, and that she didn't have the word disaster tattooed across her forehead.

"I'm not stupid," she told her sister. "I know Sam has every right to enter the competition. And I know that my entering it was more of a jog for him, a realization that he might as well give it a go. But he's so… bloody… smug and confident."

"He is a bit," Fred acknowledged. "You know he's winding you up, though, right? It's part of the mating ritual. If he were a baboon, he'd be waving his red butt in your face."

"Thank you for that image. Yeah, I get it, but it's hardly endearing me to him. Buying flowers and chocolates is also a mating ritual. Why can't he pick something like that?"

"He doesn't strike me as the flower-buying type."

"Yeah. Well, I want the flower-buying type." Frustration rang in Ginger's voice. "I deserve it, don't I? After what I've been through? I want to be romanced. I don't want some bloody scruffy local yokel thinking he's doing me a favor when he asks me out. You know what he said on Wednesday?"

"I'm afraid to ask."

"His elaborate proposal was 'the new Bourne movie is on Saturday at the cinema. You coming or what?'"

Fred stifled a laugh. "All right, I accept that's not the most romantic way to do it."

"You think? He could at least have picked a chick flick or something that didn't involve an explosion every five seconds." She sighed. "I like him, Fred, I really do, and I know he's Mac's best mate, and part of me thinks it would be such fun for us to go out and double date, but… I want more."

"All right." Fred squeezed her shoulders again. "Fair enough. He might be *hot as*, but you're right, you do deserve more." She got to her feet. "You going home now?"

"Yeah, I'm done in."

Fred paused. "Have you given any more thought to letting Phil run the place without you one day a week?"

Ginger looked out to sea. The sun had set, and the Pacific Ocean was rapidly turning from maroon to a deep, dark blue. Twilight didn't seem to exist up in the Northland—it went from day to night in what seemed like seconds. "I will soon, I promise."

"Only you're going to make yourself ill if you carry on like this. You've worked so hard, and it's time you started easing up a little. And Phil's a good guy—he'll manage."

"I'll think about it."

Fred sighed. "All right. I'll catch you tomorrow?"

"Yeah, see ya."

Ginger watched her sister head off to the big house farther up the hill that she shared with her husband, and then she turned her gaze back to the sea. The moon, half full and on the wane, hung low on the horizon like a broken china plate. It was so odd that it was upside down compared to England. She'd never get used to that.

He might be hot as… Against her will, Ginger's lips curved up at her sister's Kiwi phrase. Deep down, she had to agree with Ellie's description of him as the sexy baker. Whenever he was around, her heart beat a little a faster, and the sun shone a little brighter. But his insouciance grated on her, as well as his arrogant assumption that if he would only continue to ask her out, she'd inevitably cave at some point.

He'd also told her in no uncertain terms that he was going to win the Bay of Islands Gold Food Award, and although she accepted that he seemed to enjoy winding her up on purpose, she suspected that deep down he believed his own words. Well, waving his red butt in her face was going to get him nowhere. Ginger had given up men over a year ago, and it would take a lot more than the muffin man—no matter how sexy he was—to convince her to get back in the saddle.

About The Author

Serenity Woods is a USA Today bestselling author. She lives in the sub-tropical Northland of New Zealand with her wonderful husband and gorgeous teenage son. She writes hot and sultry contemporary romances with a happy ever after, and would much rather immerse herself in reading or writing romance than do the dusting and ironing, which is why it's not a great idea to pop round if you have any allergies.

She is the author of over fifty romance novels. You can check them all out on her website.

> Website: http://www.serenitywoodsromance.com
> Facebook: http://www.facebook.com/serenitywoodsromance
> Twitter: https://twitter.com/Serenity_Woods

Printed in Great Britain
by Amazon